Orion O'Brien
and the Spirit of Quindaro

Readers are encouraged to go to www.MissionPointPress.com to contact the author or to find information on how to buy this book in bulk at a discounted rate.

Published by Mission Point Press
2554 Chandler Rd.
Traverse City, MI 49696
(231) 421-9513
www.MissionPointPress.com

ISBN 978-1-958363-65-2
Library of Congress Control Number 2023900844

Printed in the United States of America

As an author of more than two dozen books, I have had plenty of opportunities to read. Rarely have I enjoyed reading a book as much as I enjoyed Fran Borin's first effort, Orion O'Brien and the Ghost of Samuel Grayhawk. *I'm not exactly in the demographic that Fran targeted, but I couldn't put it down. When I found out that she was releasing another book, I couldn't wait to read it. I read* Orion O'Brien and the Spirit of Quindaro *almost entirely in one sitting. If you like fiction with a lot of historical facts to back it up, you'll love reading Orion O'Brien's latest adventure. Just don't make any plans for the rest of your day!*

DAVID SMALE
Author

I like this book because it's very adventurous and because the ghost is connected to the first book. I like it because it's packed with history of the Underground Railroad.

ISAAC YOUNG
age 10, Shawnee, Kansas

Orion O'Brien, once again, discovers history through an appearance from the spirit world. This leads to investigating diaries, historical facts and listening to an elder's memories. "The Spirit of Quindaro" brings to life the Underground Railroad and its traveler's challenges. An entertaining and informative book for young readers.

NANCY WALLERSTEIN,
Former Chair of the Shawnee Indian Mission Foundation and Member, Johnson County Museum Advisory Council

ORION O'BRIEN
AND THE SPIRIT OF QUINDARO

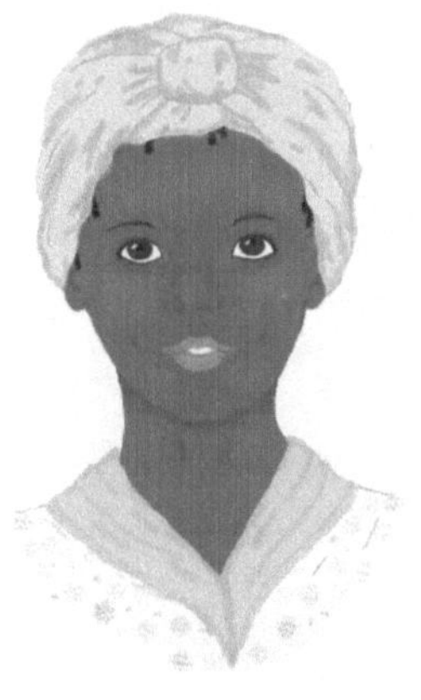

FRAN BORIN

MISSION POINT PRESS

For Phoebe

Prologue

**Western Missouri, near the border with
Bleeding Kansas: 1860**

Susanna opened her eyes sleepily as she felt someone shaking her shoulder. She started to protest, but her
mother's soothing voice urged her to be still. As Susanna
came fully awake, her mother gently pulled her up from
the straw pallet and laid her sister's old buckskin boots
in her lap. "Put 'em on and follow me," she whispered.

It was pitch-dark in the cabin, but they made their
way soundlessly out through the half-open door, and
Susanna got her bearings in the moonlight. She could
just make out her mother putting her finger to her lips
as she took Susanna by the hand and led the way down
toward the creek. They moved on, keeping toward the
edge of the fields nearest the water.

Susanna knew they'd gone at least a mile—she recognized the half-dead cottonwood tree near the north forty—before her mother turned and put her hands on her shoulders.

"I needs y'all to be real brave," said her mother. "We's gonna get away to the north, but we gotta keep quiet so's nobody hears us."

"You mean we's runnin' away?" asked Susanna. "But Mama, what if they catch us? I'm scared!"

"Shhh!" said Mama. "I knows y'all's scared...but we's gettin' away from here while we got a chance."

"But what about Daddy, and Sally and Jimmy and—"

"Daddy's comin' north soon as he can," said Mama. "You and me's leadin' the way."

"But how do you know where to go?" asked Susanna. "What if we get lost?"

Mama pointed to the sky, where countless stars twinkled in silence. "See that one star, up there?" she asked. "We just keep goin' toward that star, and we'll get to the north. We gonna walk at night and sleep in the day. When we make it to the north, we'll find somebody to help us."

Susanna felt ready to cry as she heard crickets and tree-frogs and a distant owl. "Why can't we just stay with the Chases, and we can all be together?" she whimpered.

"Cause we ain't gonna be slaves no more," said Mama. "Ain't nobody gonna sell no more of my babies, never!"

Mama wrapped a shawl around Susanna's shoulders and, step by step, they walked on through the moonlit night.

Northeast Kansas:
Present Day

Chapter 1
The Attic

Orion O'Brien, girl ghost magnet—that's me. No, really! Hey, I didn't even believe in ghosts a few months ago. Then I met Samuel Grayhawk...that is, his ghost. OK, I didn't technically *attract* Samuel. He showed up in the Martellis' basement across the street...but that's another story. So what are the chances I'd meet *another* one?! Well, as my mom says, things happen for a reason. I guess that's why it rained on Monday of spring break.

"Mom! It's *raining!* Spring break's supposed to be sunny and warm!" I whined. My brother Ollie and I had had high hopes for the week off school—Ollie wanted to practice on the Ninja Warrior challenges Dad had put up in the back yard, and I wanted to train our dog Butterscotch to run an obstacle course. Not only that, my two BFFs were out of town for the week. "I'm gonna be stuck in the house with Ollie! I wish I could've gone to Florida with Mady!"

"Cut the drama," said Mom, as Ollie made like playing a violin. "Mady will be back on Friday, and you'll get to sleep over. You'll survive until then. Besides, Sal and Sofi are staying in town, too."

"Yeah, I know." Our neighbors, Sal and Sofi Martelli, had moved in from New Jersey last summer. We all had a super adventure with Samuel Grayhawk, but lately Sal and I have been going our separate ways. He's a good guy and all, but not nearly as mature as my girlfriends and me. "Sofi's coming over this afternoon, but what am I supposed to do the rest of the week?"

"*I'm* gonna have fun," said Ollie. "Sal's teaching me to pitch, and I'm working on my Ninja Warrior moves. I'll have the whole week to practice!"

I laughed out loud. "*Your* Ninja warrior moves? Uh, like falling in the water? At least you'll already be wet from the rain." Ollie's not exactly ready for Las Vegas.

"I know it's tough about the weather," said Mom. "Tell you what—Grandpa Louie and Grandma Libby are going to start cleaning out Granny Bets's house this week. I'll bet they'd take you with them. You could take some things to do, and even help out some."

Granny Bets is my Grandpa Louie's mother, and she's like 100 years old. A few weeks ago she moved out of her old house and in with my grandma and grandpa, so they can get her house ready to sell.

Ugh. I've only been to Granny's house a few times, but I could never wait to leave. It's in an older part of town, across the county line in Kansas City, Kansas. It's ancient and dark and gloomy with lots of flowery wallpaper and old, creaky furniture. But…I love my grandma and grandpa. They're really good to us, and they helped Samuel Grayhawk get to the spirit world…even though they didn't know it. So, Ollie and I went with them to Granny's house for the morning. I packed my colored pencils and drawing pad, and Ollie took a case of Legos.

At first we helped Grandma and Grandpa clean out some kitchen cupboards. I'd never seen so much old stuff! We filled boxes and trash bags with things to either donate or throw out. Then Grandma said we could take a break, so we took our backpacks and went upstairs to find a good place to hang out.

The second floor had three bedrooms and a bathroom. Two of the bedrooms were full of old furniture and boxes. The third one used to be Granny's bedroom. There wasn't much in it—a bed frame, an old wooden chest and a box that looked like a big suitcase with the name "HAWTHORN" in yellow letters on top at the foot of the bed. Ollie flipped open the top and poked at the old clothes piled inside. A cloud of dust floated up.

"Gross!" I said. "Looks like a lot of old junk to me."

"I don't want to play here," said Ollie as he closed the box. We started to go back downstairs, when we saw another door almost hidden in shadows at the end of the hallway. Ollie ran over and tried the doorknob. It opened to more stairs.

"There must be an attic!" I said. "I never noticed this before…let's check it out!"

The stairway was narrow and dark, but we saw light coming from above. We stomped up the steps, making a racket, and I guess we kicked up a lot of dust, because I sneezed after a few steps. That's when we heard a loud C-R-R-EAK!

"Whoa!" cried Ollie. "What was that?"

"How should I know?" I said. "What do you think, there's a vampire up there or something? Don't be such a baby!"

"I'm not!" he said. "Maybe it was a branch scraping on the window?"

"It's just a creaky old house," I said. "Come on!"

The steps opened right into a room at the top of the house. The side walls sloped down from the top, and there was a little window in the front with the curtains closed. There was no ceiling, just boards across the top a few inches above my head. A bare light bulb was fixed to one of the rafters with a string hanging from it. I pulled the string and the light came on.

"What is this place?" asked Ollie. It wasn't very

big—not even as big as Ollie's room at home, and he has the smallest one—but it was decked out like a bedroom. There was a low bed with a quilt on it and a rickety-looking wooden rocking chair with some slats missing from the back. A small humpback chest sat at the foot of the bed. A long, tall mirror stood in one corner, and there were a couple of old rugs on the floor. I expected it to be dusty like the stairway, but the wood planks of the floor seemed pretty clean. When I opened the curtains, the room actually looked kind of homey.

"We can play up here!" I said. "I'll sit in the rocking chair to draw, and you can put your Legos on the rug."

"Hey, look at this!" said Ollie, running to the mirror. It wasn't like any mirror I'd ever seen. It stood by itself on wooden legs and was as tall as me. The glass was old and wavy-looking, with dark spots and lines in it. Ollie stood in front of it, waving his arms and dancing around. I went and stood by him, and we laughed at how we looked—it was sort of like a fun-house mirror. Our legs were crooked and our heads were long and skinny. There was even one dark spot where, if Ollie stood just right, he looked like he had a black eye. We were juking around to see how funny we looked, when I saw something move at the edge of the mirror. I froze. I mean it, I froze—I felt cold air on my arms, and in the mirror I saw—I swear!—a woman standing at my shoulder, looking right at us!

Chapter 2
Who's in the Mirror?

"Look!" I cried. I grabbed Ollie's arm.

Ollie stopped laughing and looked closer. The woman looked wavy and weird, like us. "Who's that?" he cried. "How did she get here?"

We whirled around, but there was nobody behind us. We turned to face the mirror again, and there she was, just looking at us. Even in the wavy mirror, we could see her pretty well. Looking closer, I saw she was really just a young girl, maybe about my age. Her skin was deep brown and her black hair was pulled back in little braids that poked out from under a thick scarf. She wore a dress with a long skirt and what looked like leather boots. All her clothes looked old and faded. She didn't smile or say anything. I turned around again to make sure there was no one there, then looked back at Ollie, who for a change, said nothing.

"We're out of here," I said. We hurried down the steps to the second floor and closed the hall door behind us. "So what did we just see?" I whispered to Ollie.

"There was a lady in the mirror," he whispered back. "But she wasn't really there!"

Now that we were out of the attic, I could hear Grandma and Grandpa moving around and talking downstairs, and I felt a little silly. My mom says there's always a logical explanation for things, we just have to figure out what it is, right?

"You were scared, I know it!" said Ollie. "Who's a baby now?"

"Shut up! Why should I be scared of her?" I said. "She just surprised me."

We stood there a minute listening to Grandpa and Grandma downstairs, and I wondered if my eyes had been playing tricks on me. How could we see something in the mirror that wasn't there? "Let's just sneak back up and look in," I said. We tiptoed back up the steps and stopped with our heads just above the floor so we could see into the attic. At first it looked exactly like it did when we left. My sketch pad and Ollie's Legos were on the rug by the mirror. Then I heard Ollie suck in his breath.

"Look at the chair!" he whispered. Sure enough, the

rocking chair was moving—just a little, like somebody just got out of it and it was still rocking. I looked all around the room. There was no mysterious girl. I went quietly up the last few steps and sat on the bed.

"So who was that up here?" I asked.

"Uh, a Black lady, or maybe a girl, wearing a long dress?" said Ollie.

"Well, Granny Bets is Black," I said. "Maybe one of her friends was staying here with her and hasn't moved out yet."

"And she was sitting in the chair and heard us coming up the stairs," said Ollie.

"But why didn't we see her when we first went up? And where did she go? She didn't go down the steps," I said. "Is there another way out?"

"Maybe there's a closet or something," said Ollie. "She could have jumped in real fast when she heard us." We went around the room, checking the walls, but didn't find any doors or hiding places. Ollie even looked under the bed.

"And why couldn't we *see* her? We only saw her in the mirror, but not for real!" I said. "And did you feel it get colder right when she showed up?"

"Uh, I'm not sure," said Ollie.

"Besides, did she look like a normal person to you?" I asked.

"Not really," said Ollie. "I mean, she looked more

like somebody from a long time ago, the way she was dressed."

He was right. That's when it hit me. I almost didn't want to say the words, but… "Well…what if she was? From a long time ago, I mean?"

"What? Are you cra…o-o-o-h! You mean…like Samuel? A…a *ghost*?" said Ollie.

"SHHH! Not so loud!" I warned. "But think about it. Do you see real people in mirrors when they're not really there?" We started down the steps.

"Are we gonna tell Grandma and Grandpa?" asked Ollie.

"Are you serious?" I said. "They'll think we *are* crazy."

We heard Grandma Libby calling us and ran down to the kitchen.

"Did you find a good place to play?" she asked. "I thought I heard you go up to the attic."

"There's not much up there, so we had plenty of room for our stuff," I said, giving Ollie the evil eye to make sure he kept quiet. I wanted to change the subject. "What's that big box in Granny's room? The one that says 'Hawthorn' on it?"

"That was your great-grandpa's footlocker from the Army," she said. "It's been all the way to Belgium and back. We'll take it home for Granny later this week."

"The Army?" asked Ollie. He goes gaga over anything

that has to do with soldiers and fighting. "It looked like just a bunch of dusty old clothes."

"Well, remember, it belongs to Granny," said Grandma. "Right now we've got the van loaded, and we need to make a trip to the donation center."

"Did you turn off the light in the attic?" asked Grandpa before he locked up the house.

Ollie and I looked at each other. "We left our stuff up there," I said. Ollie didn't move, so I pulled him by the arm toward the stairs. "Who's afraid now?" I whispered as we got to the landing.

"Not me!" said Ollie. He ran up the attic staircase ahead of me. The attic light was still on. I followed him up to the room and reached for the string to turn off the light. Something was…different. My eyes fell on the rocking chair, and there sitting propped up against the back was an old doll. I put my finger to my lips and pointed to the doll. Ollie's eyes almost popped out when he saw it. We grabbed our things and hustled down the steps as fast as we could.

Chapter 3
A Tall Tale?

As soon as Grandpa dropped us off at home, I said to Ollie, "We have to tell Sal and Sofi about this! This'll blow them away!"

Sal and Sofi are the only two people in the world, besides Ollie and me, who know about Samuel Grayhawk…that is, who know he was a ghost. In case you don't remember, Samuel was a Wyandot Indian boy who went to school at the Shawnee Indian Mission back in the 1840s. When his sister was dying, he jumped on a horse to go see her, but the horse threw him off. He crawled into a cellar and died, and no one ever found him. Years later, Sal and Sofi's house was built over the place where he died. And we just happened to find him in their basement.

We got to be really good friends with Samuel, and we had so much fun, but he had to find where his sister was buried so he could join her in the spirit world. We did our best to help him. My grandparents and our neighbors helped a lot, too. But nobody else knew he was a ghost.

"Yeah, I'm going with Sal up to the schoolyard after lunch to practice pitching. I can tell him then!" said Ollie.

"No, you don't!" I said as we went in the front door. I had plans of my own for the afternoon, but I wasn't going to miss the big reveal. "If you tell him before I get there, you're dead!"

"What don't you want him to tell?" asked my mom, who came to meet us at the door.

I had to think fast. "Uh…that I'm going to color my hair!" I said. "I want it to be a surprise!" Ollie rolled his eyes.

"Oh, it'll be a surprise all right," said Mom. "Come on, lunch is ready. Tell me what you did at Granny's house."

The rain had stopped, so Ollie went with Sal to the school playground to practice pitching. Sal's in fifth grade like me, but he's a few months younger (and a whole lot shorter). He treats Ollie kinda like a little brother, and Sofi tags along with me sometimes to do girl things.

Getting rid of Ollie for a while was perfect. I'd gotten a hair coloring kit for my eleventh birthday a couple of weeks earlier. Mom was going to help me color my hair that afternoon, and the last thing I needed was my brother making stupid comments.

"Remember, don't tell him about the girl in the mirror before I get there," I warned as he went out the door to meet Sal.

I'd invited Sofi over to watch. She's in second grade, a year behind Ollie. She's been doing gymnastics since she was four, and she's pretty darn good. I think that's one of the reasons Ollie's gotten into the Ninja Warrior thing—he wants to be good at something, too. Sofi's the perfect little sister—real quiet, but always ready to do whatever the rest of us are doing. Too bad I can't trade Ollie for Sofi….

I wore one of Dad's old T-shirts and sat on a stool in front of the mirror while Mom put the color in. My hair's long and curly and honey-brown, and I wanted some streaks of pink and yellow and aqua blue. I thought it'd look good for spring, and I was saving the purple for a special occasion, like maybe the last day of school. It was kind of messy, but it turned out great, and Sofi loved it! After we cleaned up, Sofi and I took Butterscotch and went to find Ollie and Sal.

"Do you think they'll like it?" I asked Sofi on the way. She just giggled and nodded. When we got to the schoolyard, Sal and Ollie were talking to a couple of neighborhood boys.

"Yikes!" said Ollie when he saw me. "I didn't know you were gonna do stripes!"

"What do you think?" I asked. I turned my head so they could see it all.

"You look like a troll," said one of the boys. "The ones with the big, googly eyes and wrinkly faces." I shook my hair in the boy's face. He's only a fourth-grader, so who cares what he thinks?

"Umm…it's really bright," said Sal. "Are you going to school like that?"

"Nope, Mom says I have to wash it out before next week. But I might do it again for the last day of school!"

"Let's go!" cried Ollie. "You've gotta hear what we saw this morning!" He was dying to tell Sal about the girl in the mirror.

"Not so loud!" I said. "Wait till we get closer to our house!"

"So, what is it?" asked Sal as we left the playground. "It must be something really good or really bad."

"Well," I began, "we went with my grandparents to clean out our Granny Bets's house, and we found this old wavy mirror—"

"And we saw a ghost in the mirror!" Ollie interrupted. He just can't help himself sometimes.

Sal threw his ball in the air and caught it. "You didn't see any ghost! What do you think I am, six years old?"

"Honest, we saw a girl in the mirror, but she wasn't really there!" said Ollie.

"Ollie, shut up for a minute," I said. "It was like a fun-house mirror, that makes you look all crazy, and we were looking in it, and we saw a girl looking around from behind us. But when we turned around to see her, she wasn't there!"

Sal looked at us for a second and then busted out laughing. "Are you *serious*? It was just a wavy place in the mirror!" he said. "I've seen those mirrors before, and they do weird things. It probably just made you look double."

"Uh…no," I said. "She was wearing old-fashioned clothes, and she was Black."

"Exactly!" said Sal. "You're part Black." He knows my Grandpa Louie is African-American. "It was your own reflection!" He was having way too much fun with this.

"Honest, we saw a Black lady, or girl maybe, in the mirror, and she wore old-fashioned clothes and had a cloth on her head," said Ollie.

"Then there really was somebody there, but she went away, real fast," said Sal. "So what?"

"There was nobody in the room but us!" I said.

"No way," said Sal. He didn't believe a word of it. "She got away before you saw where she went…or maybe you just saw something that *looked* like a girl."

"Like what?" I asked.

Sal shrugged. "I don't know…a doll? A statue? One of those things like in store windows with clothes on them."

Aarrgghh! Why didn't Sal believe me? By this time we were at our back yard, so I ducked into the house to get a treat for Butterscotch. I saw a pan of brownies on the kitchen counter and grabbed them too. When I got back outside, Ollie was showing off the Ninja Warrior course. It had floating steps we'd made by putting two basketballs and two soccer balls in a line on the ground with some boards to keep them in place. Sal and Sofi tried it out.

Then Ollie showed off his flying trapeze move. He climbed the ladder to our tree house. It's really just a big piece of wood you can sit or stand on, with a rope that comes down from a higher branch. There's a metal bar hanging from another branch, like a trapeze, and Ollie's been trying to swing from the rope and jump to the bar. As usual, he missed the bar and landed on the ground.

"You have to be higher on the rope," said Sal.

"So, about the girl in the mirror," I said. "Why would I make this up?" I held a dog treat in front of Butterscotch to get her to weave in and out of some poles we'd stuck in the ground. "Good girl!" I said. I gave her the treat and looked back at Sal. I couldn't believe he was blowing us off.

"I don't know," said Sal. "It just doesn't seem possible, is all. Did you ask your grandpa if anybody else lives in the house?"

"No," I said. "Why would they be cleaning it out if somebody else lived there?"

"I think she *used to* live there," said Ollie. "The attic looks like a bedroom, like where she lived when she was alive." He was in the tree house again, ready to swing and grab the trapeze bar. He missed again.

"Get real!" said Sal. "So, somebody used to live in your granny's attic—big deal. I'll bet there's a picture of her hanging on the wall, and that's what you saw in the mirror."

"There's no picture on the wall! But remember? Samuel could appear and disappear when he wanted to," I said.

"And that's not all," said Ollie as he stuffed a brownie in his mouth. "We saw the rocking chair moving, and then when we went up to turn the light off, there was a doll on the chair that wasn't there before!"

"And," I said, "right when she showed up in the mirror, it got real cold."

"Why didn't you go right then and tell your grandpa?" Sal asked. "Weren't you scared?"

"Well…it *was* pretty weird," I said. "But then I just thought, okay, we've seen a ghost before, and nothing bad happened to us, so I wanted to check it out. Besides, if you don't believe me, why do you think my grandpa would?"

"I don't know," said Sal, shaking his head. "There's gotta be some explanation! I mean, sure, we found Samuel's ghost and all, but that was a one-off—it's never gonna happen again."

"Oh, now *you're* the one with the logical explanation? You sound like my mom—and me, before we met Samuel!" I said. "I'm the one who never believed in ghosts, and you went around talking about haunted houses! But I'll bet the girl we saw today was a ghost. Think about it...what if we could talk to her like we did with Samuel! That would be so cool!"

"Why don't you come and see for yourself?" asked Ollie.

"Good idea," I said. "We can go again tomorrow, and if we don't see her, we'll never say another word about it."

Sal shrugged. "Why not? I *don't* really believe it, but what have I got to lose?"

Chapter 4
Secrets in the Locker

It rained again the next morning, and Mrs. Martelli said Sal and Sofi could go with us to Granny's as long as they didn't make a mess or track mud in the house. They came over to wait with us for Grandma and Grandpa to pick us up. Ollie wanted to take Butterscotch, which was a good idea. Remember how Butterscotch had sensed that something—or someone—was in the Martellis' basement before we ever had a clue about Samuel? But we couldn't exactly say we needed her to sniff out a ghost. Anyway, Mom said four kids were enough for Grandma and Grandpa to deal with.

Sal had some cards and games in his backpack. "I'm not real sure this 'ghost' girl's gonna show up," he said, "so I'm bringing some stuff to do."

I knew he still didn't believe we'd seen the girl in the mirror. I just hoped she would be there again.

Grandpa pulled the old van into the driveway and we ran to get in.

"Is this the latest hair fashion?" asked Grandma when I pulled my hood off and she saw my streaks.

"I always knew you were a bright girl!" said Grandpa.

"Kind of like a clown, if you ask me," said Ollie.

"Nobody asked you," I said. I told Grandma and Grandpa we wanted to show Sal and Sofi the playroom we'd discovered in the attic.

We drove up close to the front porch of Granny's house to try to stay out of the rain. Just as Grandpa was turning off the engine, Sofi cried out, "Look!" I turned to where she was pointing, and saw a kitten huddling on the porch. I threw my hood over my head and ran to get it.

We brought the kitten inside to the kitchen. It had white fur with black and orange patches all over it, and it was really wet. Sofi latched onto it right away. "Is it a boy or a girl?" she asked.

"It's a girl," said Grandma. "See her colors? That's called calico, and calico cats are always girls."

"Can we keep her?" asked Sofi.

"We'll need to find out if she belongs to someone," said Grandma. "She doesn't have a collar or a tag, but if she's lost, somebody might be wondering where she is." She got out some old towels and Sofi dried the kitten off while the rest of us filled boxes with old pots, pans and dishes. I was antsy to get to the attic, but we couldn't just run off without helping.

After about an hour, Grandma said we could go play, so we took Sal and Sofi, and the kitten, up the attic stairs. I'm the tallest, so a few steps before the top, I looked around the room. I had my sketch pad with me, so if the girl came back, I could draw a picture of her. If I'd gotten a phone last Christmas like I wanted, I could just take a photo, but...oh, well.

"Coast's clear," I said, and we all hurried up the last few steps. Ollie ran straight for the mirror, and started dancing around, acting crazy. Sofi, holding the kitten, danced beside him.

"This place is really old," said Sal, looking around the room. "What's that?"

He was pointing to the rocking chair. The old doll was still there. It wasn't like any doll I'd ever had. It was made out of cloth and had black yarn hair, and wore a faded dress. Its face was stitched on with colored thread. It looked shabby and worn, but the stitching on the face was neat and nice. I picked it up and sat down slowly in the chair. As I leaned back, the chair gave a loud C-R-EAK!

"That's the sound we heard yesterday!" cried Ollie. "I'll bet somebody was sitting there and got up when they heard us coming!"

Sal gave him a look. "You can't be serious, dude," he said.

"That's where we saw her," I said. I got up from the chair and pointed to the edge of the mirror. I was still holding the doll.

"Oh, sweet! It's like a fun-house mirror!" said Sal, mugging and moving around like a maniac. That's when I felt the air around me turning cold, and I looked at the edge of the mirror, expecting to see the girl. There was nothing there, but I felt something moving beside me and before I knew it, the doll flew out of my hand and landed back on the chair.

"Wow!" cried Ollie. "How'd you do that?"

All I could do was look from my empty hand to the chair. I finally sputtered, "Did...did you see that?"

Sal looked over at me. He'd been clowning in the mirror and hadn't seen anything, but Sofi and Ollie's eyes were popping out.

"See what?" asked Sal. "What's everybody looking at?"

"Orion just launched the doll into the chair from over here!" said Ollie. "Nice move!"

I stood there, shaking my head, and said, "I didn't... it flew over there on its own!"

"Will you cut the crap?" said Sal. "I didn't see anything—"

CR-R-EA-K! This time it wasn't the chair, but a

floorboard that creaked. Everybody stopped talking. The kitten jumped out of Sofi's arms, leaped over to the chair, and arched her back. She let out a tiny yowl.

Ollie and Sofi jumped up, and Sofi scooped up the kitten. I was still freaked from the doll flying out of my hand and was almost ready to run down the steps.

"What's wrong with you?" asked Sal. "It's just a creaky board, that's all."

"Will you just listen?" I said. "I felt something moving beside me and the doll flew out of my hand! I didn't throw it or anything! Then the floor creaked, like somebody stepped on a loose board."

Sal cracked up. "You should see your face! You look like you saw a ghost!" he laughed. "Look, this floor's ancient, all the boards are probably loose! I don't believe you guys!"

"The kitten knew there was something there," said Sofi.

"Yeah, you saw how she jumped out of Sofi's arms," said Ollie. "It's like how Butterscotch acted when she knew Samuel was in your basement, even though we couldn't see him!"

"You guys are whacked," said Sal. "Nobody's been up here for a hundred years! And where's this girl in the mirror? I came all the way here to see a ghost, and all you can show me is a ragged old doll?"

"She was here! Ollie and I both saw her!" I cried.

I was getting upset. The girl wasn't in the mirror, and Sal didn't believe me, and nothing was working out the way I wanted. "I just don't understand! Yesterday, she showed up as soon as Ollie and I looked in the mirror... so why won't she do it now?"

"Just chill," said Sal. "I like it up here...come on, I brought my Monopoly Junior."

I TRIED TO FORGET ABOUT the girl in the mirror and have fun playing the game, but I felt pretty let down. I'd started to believe we might have another cool adventure, like we had with Samuel. Now all I wanted was to go home.

As soon as I ran out of Monopoly money, I stood up. "I'm going down to Granny's old room," I said. "Maybe I'll check out the old footlocker. You guys can stay here if you want."

I'd barely gotten to Granny's room and pulled the footlocker to the middle of the floor when I heard the others clattering down the stairs. Ollie dropped onto the floor beside me and said, "Sofi put the kitten down and she messed up the Monopoly board, so we decided to quit. Besides, Sal was beating everybody." Sal and Sofi sat down, too.

"What's in there?" asked Sal.

"It's my great-grandpa's old Army footlocker," I said. "Grandma said he had it in Belgium."

"Let's look in," said Sal.

Ollie, who always has to be first, opened the lid and stuck his arm right down into the dusty locker, under the stuff on top. He pulled out an old cardboard box that rattled when he shook it. When he pulled off the top, we saw what looked like medals. One was a heart shape with a purple ribbon on it, and another was a gold star with a red, white and blue ribbon. There was also a cloth patch with a snarling panther on it.

"Wow!" cried Ollie. "What are these?"

"Those look like war medals," said Sal. "I'm pretty sure that's a Purple Heart. Was your great-grandpa in a war?"

I shrugged. "I guess so," I said. "He died before I was born."

"I'm gonna take them down and ask Grandpa about them!" said Ollie. You would've thought he'd discovered gold or something.

Sal pulled out the dusty coat that was on top. "This must be his Army uniform," he said. "Maybe your great-grandpa was a war hero!"

Under the coat was a small old book. It was full of handwriting. I thumbed through a few of the pages, but the ink was all faded and the writing was *really* hard to read. Inside the front cover I could make out the words "Mattie Briggs 1889."

"Looks like a diary," I said. "But who is Mattie

Briggs?" I put the book back into the locker. I could ask Grandpa later who Mattie was.

Sofi picked up a little bundle of tissue paper and unwrapped it. There was a harmonica inside. The metal was dull and dented, not shiny and clean-looking, but Ollie put it up to his mouth anyway.

"There's probably a zillion dead spiders in there!" I said. Ollie dropped the harmonica.

Nothing else in the locker looked very interesting— photos of people I didn't recognize, some old papers, and a few books. We put everything back inside except for the box of medals.

"Let's go ask Grandpa about these," said Ollie, shaking the box. "I want to know if my great-grandpa was a war hero!"

"OK," I said. I was still bummed that the girl hadn't shown up in the mirror, but what could I do about it? I was starting to get up off the floor when I heard something. The floor above our heads began creaking again.

Chapter 5

Footsteps...a Voice...and a Face

"Listen!" I cried. "Did you hear that?" Everybody stopped moving and got quiet. After a few seconds, the floor creaked again. Sal looked toward the ceiling, so I knew he heard it too.

"It sounds like somebody walking in the attic!" shouted Ollie.

We sat where we were for what seemed like ages, but it was probably just a minute. We didn't hear any more footsteps.

"Your grandma or grandpa probably went up there," said Sal. "Nothing weird about that. Come on, I want to hear about the medals, too."

"We would have seen or heard them if they went up there!" I said. Why was Sal being such a butthead about this? I followed the others out of Granny's room to the hallway, but I couldn't resist sticking my head into the attic stairway one more time before going down. That's when I heard the singing.

"Listen!" I whispered. Everyone came and leaned into the stairway. A soft voice was singing what sounded like...a lullaby.

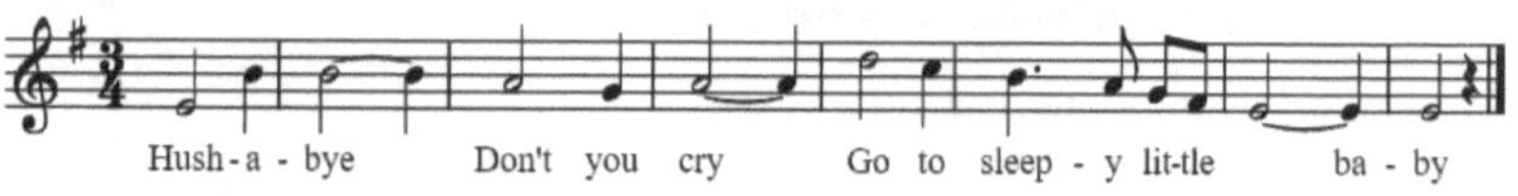

"That's just your grandma singing," said Sal.

"It is not!" said Ollie. "That doesn't sound like Grandma!"

"I'm going up to see, even if you're not," I whispered. "I saw the girl yesterday and she didn't hurt me, and I'm not afraid to go back." I started tiptoeing up the steps. Sal, Sofi and Ollie were right behind me. The singing got louder as we went up, but a few steps from the top, Ollie coughed. The singing stopped. We went on, one step at a time, until our heads poked up above the floor. No one was in the room, but the rocking chair was moving, just a little. Monopoly money and game pieces were scattered around on the floor, but the doll was gone. Without a word we all rushed into the room and looked around.

"Where's the doll?" asked Ollie.

"In there," said Sal, looking over at the humpback chest by the bed. The top of the chest was propped open and we could see the doll laying on top of some other things. As Sal started to reach for it, the top slammed shut with a bang! He jumped back.

"Whoa!" said Sal. "That thing tried to take my fingers off!"

"It's the girl we saw in the mirror," I said. "I guess she doesn't want you messing with her stuff!"

"See?" said Ollie. "We know she's here, because the doll was on the chair when we left, and now it's in the chest!"

"OK, you guys," I said. "Let's just sit down and see what happens."

We sat on the floor in front of the mirror. Nobody said a word. We waited a few minutes, but there was no cold air or creaking floorboards. Finally, Sal and Ollie started making stupid faces and laughing, and Sofi joined in, holding the kitten up to the mirror. That's when I felt the cold air on my arms. I looked at the edge of the mirror, and there she was—the Black girl with old-fashioned clothes and a scarf over her head, leaning over behind us. She seemed to be looking at the kitten.

"Look!" cried Sofi, and we all stared at the girl. Ollie shivered a little and rubbed his arms to keep warm.

"What the…?" said Sal. I turned around to make sure there wasn't anybody in the room with us, and Sal did the same. But Sofi scooted closer to the mirror and held the kitten's paw up for a little wave.

"Hi," said Sofi. The girl looked at the kitten like she wanted to hold it. Then she disappeared. We all looked around again, just to make sure we weren't dreaming.

"Now do you believe me?" I asked Sal.

He looked back at me and slowly nodded. "Un-freaking-believable! But where'd she go? She was here one second and gone the next!"

Right then I heard Grandma Libby calling from downstairs. "Kids! Come on, time for lunch! We'll go to McDonalds!"

We all scrambled down the stairs.

When we got in the car, Ollie opened the box to show Grandpa the medals.

"Yep, those are my dad's," said Grandpa. "He was a tank gunner in Belgium in World War II, in the first all-Black tank regiment in the U.S. Army. He got a Purple Heart and a Silver Star."

"Isn't the Purple Heart for getting wounded?" asked Sal.

"That's right," said Grandpa. "He took a bullet in the arm. He was proud of his regiment, but he never liked to talk about the war much."

"That is so awesome!" cried Ollie. "My great-grandpa got wounded in the war!"

"I doubt if he thought it was awesome," said Grandma Libby.

"Can I keep them?" asked Ollie.

"They belong to Granny," said Grandpa. "You can look at them for now, but then put them back in the locker."

"Grandpa, who's Mattie Briggs?" I asked. "There's an old diary in the locker, and it has her name in it."

"That's one of Granny's grandmas," said Grandpa Louie. "I think she was one of the first ones in our family to settle in this area. You should probably ask Granny to tell you."

"So," said Sal to Grandpa, "Orion's great-grandma is your mom, right? Is she really 100 years old?"

Grandpa laughed. "Seems like it to you, I'll bet, but she's only 94. She hated to leave that house, but she needs to be with us in case she falls or needs help."

"How long did she live there?" I asked.

"Oh, 35 or 40 years, at least," Grandpa said.

I zoned out while they talked, thinking about Granny Bets. The truth is, I really don't know much about her. I only see her like at holidays, and she's nice, I guess, but she mostly talks to the grown-ups. Nobody's ever said there's anything strange about her or her house.

"Do you think she'd like it if we went to visit her?" I asked.

"That's a good idea," said Grandma Libby. "You know, Granny won't live forever. She loves to see you, and you could ask her about the diary and the family history."

Yeah, I thought. *I wonder what she really knows...*

Chapter 6
A Message From the Spirit

When we got back, Sofi fed the kitten some bits of hamburger she'd saved. The kitten scarfed it all down.

"We should name her," said Ollie.

I wanted to name her Ali, like for an alley cat, but Sofi kept saying, "Cali-co-co! Cali-co-co!" so we decided to call her Coco.

We were all dying to go back to the attic, but Grandma asked us to clean out the closet by the front door. Ollie and Sofi were supposed to be helping, but they mostly played with Coco, so Sal and I did all the work. Grandpa was doing something in the cellar, and Grandma was taking curtains down all over the house, which gave us a chance to discuss the girl in the mirror.

"Why can't we see her?" I asked. "Except in the

mirror? She can't really be *inside* the mirror, 'cause she does stuff out in the room. She grabbed the doll out of my hand, and we know she sits in the chair."

"And she slammed the chest shut when I tried to look in!" said Sal.

"But she's invisible!" I said.

Ollie looked up. "Samuel was invisible most of the time," he said.

"So maybe she just doesn't want us to see her," said Sal. "Outside the mirror, I mean."

"But that doesn't make sense!" I said. "She knows we see her in the mirror. It's like...she can't get out...like she doesn't really have...a *body*."

Sal thought a minute. "Maybe that's right. Samuel could show up in his body if he wanted. There must be some reason she can't do that."

"Or won't," I said. "But why did she let us see her at all? She could have just stayed invisible, and we'd never have a clue she was there...it's like she's playing a game."

"Maybe she wants something from us," said Ollie.

"Hmmm," said Sal. "Like what?"

We finished packing up the closet and told Grandma we were going to wrap up our Monopoly game. We didn't hear anything going up the steps, but as soon as we got into the attic, Sal pointed at the game board.

"Look!" he cried. "Who did this?"

The money was stacked up in a neat pile in the

middle of the board with the game pieces beside it.

"She picked up the game!" said Ollie, dropping onto his knees.

"You know what?" said Sal. "She sent us a message! She made a move, and the ball's in our court now. I bet she wants to talk to us."

We pushed the game board out of the way and sat down in front of the mirror. Coco was on Sofi's lap, looking like she was ready for a nap. All of a sudden, her head snapped up. She jumped to the floor in front of Sofi and stretched her tail in the air. I felt the room turning cold. I looked up at the mirror just in time to see the mysterious Black girl standing behind us. She was looking at Coco again.

"Hi," said Sofi as she picked Coco back up. "What's your name?" She smiled up at the girl.

"Susanna," said the reflection in the mirror after a few seconds.

She talked! I stared in the mirror and saw Sal's mouth hanging open. It would have been funny if it wasn't totally bizarre! Sofi just kept smiling up at the girl.

I took a good look at the girl. She was thin but not scrawny and about as tall as me. She had smooth skin and huge dark eyes with the longest, thickest lashes I'd ever seen. She didn't look mean or angry. I closed my eyes for a second and told myself to stay calm. I could hear the vacuum cleaner running downstairs. Grandma and Grandpa were close by…what could possibly happen? And I thought about her singing…it was a lullaby, for Pete's sake! Sal was right, she must want to talk to us, or she would've just stayed away from the mirror, right? I took a deep breath.

"My name's Orion," I said.

"And I'm Ollie," said Ollie. "Orion's my sister." Sal introduced himself and Sofi, and Sofi held Coco up to the mirror again.

"Ain't seen such a pretty cat in a long time," she said. Her voice was soft, and she pronounced her words in kind of a slow, drawn-out way. She mostly looked down at the floor as she talked.

"Susanna? Don't be afraid," I said. "We just wanted to know who you are."

She looked up from under her long, dark lashes, and I decided she wasn't afraid, exactly, more like…shy. Then she did kind of a curtsy and said, "Y'all can call me Susie."

"But what are you doing here?" asked Ollie.

"This be our room," said Susie. "Mama's, and me and Rebecca's."

"Hold on, this is my Granny Bets's house!" I said. "Does she know you're here?"

Susie looked at me for a few seconds, then nodded. "Miz Bets keep the secret," she said.

"Whoa!" said Sal, looking at me. "Your great-grandma knows about this? And she never told anybody?"

"Granny Bets never told *me* anything about any secrets!" I said.

"But she must know something...." said Sal.

"Did you move in with Granny Bets?" asked Ollie.

Susie shook her head. "*She* move in with *us*. We been here since the house got built," she said. "We come here with the Armstrongs."

"The Armstrongs? Is that who built the house?" I asked. Susie nodded.

"Did my granny...Ms. Bets...ever talk to you?" asked Ollie.

"She never say nothin' to me," said Susie. "She come up the steps once in a while, poke her head in the room, but she never talk to me."

"Then how do you know she knows about you?" I asked.

"'Cause she keep our room just the same as always," said Susie.

"So why did you show up in the mirror?" asked Ollie. "Did you want to talk to us?"

"Yeah, it's like *you* came to *us*," I said. "What for?"

Susie looked up at me. "Thought you might know somethin' about my daddy," she said. "I was hopin' you come from someplace close to Mr. Chase's, over in Missouri."

"Hold it!" I said. "How would we know about your

dad? And why did you think we're from Missouri? Is that where you're from? Then how did you get here?"

"Hey!" said Sal. "Give her a chance to tell us!"

"We come on the railroad," said Susie. "Mama and me, to wait for my daddy, but he ain't got here yet. Still waitin', I am."

"Oh, cool!" said Ollie. "You rode on a train to get here?"

"Train?" said Susie, looking from Ollie to me. "Y'all know…the *underground* railroad. Ain't that how *y'all* got here?"

Sal and I had heard about the underground railroad in fifth grade history, but why would Susie think I'd come on it?

"The underground railroad?" said Ollie. "You mean a train went underground?"

Susie gave him a blank look, then said, "Y'all wasn't slaves, then?"

"What? No way!" laughed Ollie.

"Y'all got freed?" asked Susie. Ollie and I looked at each other.

"Oh. My. God," said Sal, "she thinks you guys were slaves! Look at you!"

I looked at Sal in horror as his words sank in. "Holy…!" I sputtered. I hardly knew what to say. "You mean…oh, my God, she thinks we're slaves who ran away 'cause…because…our skin's brown? Like hers!"

Chapter 7
The Spirit Speaks

I looked back at Susie. "You thought we were slaves?" I asked. "Ollie and me?"

Susie nodded. "Y'all look like runaways to me," she said. "Seen you wearin' them old boys' clothes, prob'ly to help you excape. Wanted to ask if y'all's from a farm near Mr. Chase or Mr. Briggs."

"I'm not wearing boys' clothes!" I said. Then I looked at my jeans with the holes in the knees, and my T-shirt, and realized what it might look like to Susie. "This is what I always wear."

"'Course, then I seen your hair, and didn't know what to think," said Susie.

"My hair?" I asked. "Oh, my hair! Do you like my streaks?"

"Never seen nothin' quite like it," she said. *Hmmmm…*

"We've never been slaves," I said.

"What about…them two?" she asked, looking toward Sal and then Sofi. She seemed a little nervous. "They ain't the master's children?"

I busted out laughing, but then stopped as I suddenly understood. Susie saw two brown kids and two white kids. And I realized Susie had only talked to me and Ollie, never to Sal or Sofi. If she lived at the time of the underground railroad—and slavery—she probably didn't trust white people.

"Susie, there aren't any slaves anymore. They got freed 'cause of the Civil War. And we're all friends. We go to school and play together," I said.

Susie's eyes got round. "I knowed about the war, but…y'all say the slaves got freed?!" She shook her head in wonder. "And…and *y'all* go to school!" She looked from me to Ollie.

"Yeah, we have to," said Ollie.

"But *you* were a slave, weren't you?" asked Sal excitedly. "I get it now! You got away on the underground railroad…so who are you and where did you come from?" I guess he was a true believer now!

I still wasn't sure she was going to talk to Sal, but then she lifted her chin.

"Name's Susanna Chase, and I come from Mr. Chase's farm in Missouri," she said. "Lived there with my mama and brothers and sisters. Then me and Mama runned away so's Mr. Chase couldn't sell me. He done selled away two of my brothers off to Arkansas. They was just seven and nine years old."

We all gasped. "*Seven?!*" said Sal. "That's how old Sofi is!" Sofi looked terrified.

Susie went on. "My mama's afraid Mr. Chase'll sell me, too. She and my daddy, they decided to run away so he couldn't sell no more of us. Thing is, Mama's gonna have another baby in the winter. We gotta run before the baby come. And we come here and stayed with the Armstrongs."

"You actually escaped from slavery?" said Sal. "That is unbelievable!"

"But why were you waiting for your dad?" I asked.

"My daddy live over at the Briggs farm. He and Mama don't want to run at the same time, 'cause then ever'body know they runned away. He was gonna wait a few days and then follow us."

"But he never came?" asked Ollie.

"Not never," she said. "Don't know why, if he runned and got caught, or if somethin' else happened to him on the way...."

"And you're still waiting!" I said.

"Do you realize how long it's been?" said Sal. "There haven't been any slaves for more than 150 years!" Being the math geek of Konza School, he had this figured out.

Susie's eyes got even bigger. "A hundred and fifty...I never knowed how long it was!"

I could hardly believe my ears. And wouldn't you know, right then Grandpa called us from downstairs. Bummer! We had to leave for the day, but just to make sure I was right about Susie, I had to ask one more thing—but I wasn't sure how to say it.

"Susie," I said, "It's true, slavery and the underground railroad and all, that was a long time ago, so...are you, like—" As usual, Ollie got right to the point.

"Are you dead?" he asked.

Susie looked down for a long time, and I thought she wasn't going to answer. But then she nodded, and I saw tears trickling down her cheeks.

"On account of the sickness...the measles. Took so many. Mama got it first. After she gone, I want so bad to stay alive, to take care of Rebecca...my baby sister. But then she got it, too. Miz Armstrong, she nursed us the best she can. But them measles...they's *bad*. After Rebecca died, I tried to hang on...couldn't stand to let my daddy down...but then, durin' the night, the measles got me too."

"Oh, Susie, I'm so sorry!" I said. I wanted more than anything to just hug her, but you can't hug somebody who isn't really there. Sofi was sniffling, and hugged the kitten tighter.

"I'm sorry, too," said Sal, and Ollie nodded.

"We was hopin' to get to Canada," said Susie, "'cause there ain't no slavery there. But we never got a chance."

"But why are you still here in the house?" I asked. "Didn't you get buried?"

"We got buried, me, Mama and Rebecca," said Susie. "But y'all knows how it is—I had to come back, to wait for my daddy, and I didn't have no place else to go. I would've brung Rebecca with me, 'cause he never even seen her. But I guess she's too small to make that jump outta the grave."

"Wait, you jumped out of your grave?" I asked. "How did you do it?"

Susie shrugged. "Just did it," she said.

"So you're a ghost for sure!" cried Ollie.

Susie shook her head. "Ghost? Don't know. I knows I ain't alive no more. Feels like I'm just a shadow of what I used to be."

Grandpa called us again.

"We have to go now," I said, "but we've gotta hear more about you! Will you come and talk to us again tomorrow?"

"We'll bring Coco," said Sofi, lifting the kitten to the mirror.

Susie gazed at us for a second, then did her little curtsy, and disappeared in the mirror.

"*Now* do you believe me?" I asked Sal on the way down the steps. I just couldn't resist rubbing it in a little.

"I guess you were right," he said. "I admit it."

Back downstairs, we helped Grandpa and Grandma load the van so they could lock up the house.

"Are we leaving Coco here?" asked Sofi.

"Well, we still don't know who she belongs to," said Grandma. "She might decide to go home on her own."

Sofi looked like she might cry, but she helped Grandma make a bed out of some old towels on the front porch and put out a bowl of water for the kitten. Grandpa Louie put a sign on the light pole in front of Granny's house. It said, "Found: Calico Kitten" and gave his phone number.

"Are you coming back with us in the morning?" asked Grandpa.

"Sure! We love playing in the attic!" said Ollie.

"I want to see Coco again!" cried Sofi. "I hope she's still here!"

On the way home I asked Grandpa Louie, "Did anybody else ever live there with Granny?"

"No, she was all alone after my dad passed away, and she really wanted that house," said Grandpa. "Why do you ask?"

"Oh, I just wondered," I said. What I didn't say was, *why did she really want that house?*

AFTER GRANDPA DROPPED US OFF, we took Butterscotch and went to the Martellis' basement playroom to use their computer. Sal brought a cookie jar of his mom's homemade biscotti and we sat on the beanbag chairs, eating and feeding tidbits to Butterscotch. We Googled "can you see ghosts in mirrors?" I was surprised at how many links came up. I guess it's not that unusual to have ghosts appear in mirrors. We clicked the links one by one, but they didn't help much. Some had photos that were supposed to show ghosts in mirrors, and there was even a YouTube video, but we couldn't see any ghosts in any of them.

"This stuff all looks fake," said Sal. "But we really *did* see Susie in that mirror!"

Ollie kept jumping around. "I can't think about this anymore!" he yelled. "Let's get outside before my brain explodes!"

"Good idea," said Sal. "Sometimes you do your best thinking if you don't try too hard."

Chapter 8
The Underground Railroad

The rain had mostly stopped, and Ollie and Sal headed to the schoolyard to practice pitching. Sofi and I went to our back yard with Butterscotch. I tried to take Sal's advice and stop thinking about ghosts for a while. I grabbed some dog treats from the kitchen.

Dad had fixed a hurdle with a bar that we could raise and lower for Butterscotch. I'd been trying to get her to jump over it, but she wasn't getting the idea. I tried laying the bar on the ground and holding a dog treat in front of her. She walked over the bar to get the treat.

"Good girl!" said Sofi. After that we put the bar up a little at a time, giving her treats each time she stepped over it. But when the bar was up to about six inches, she just stood there looking up at me. I held a treat above her head and yelled, "Jump, Butterscotch!" She barked at me a couple of times, and finally jumped up to get the treat! We tried it a couple more times, hugging and patting her every time she jumped.

"We've gotta show Ollie and Sal!" I said. "Let's go get 'em!"

Sofi and I headed to the school yard to find Sal and Ollie. They'd finished pitching, and Ollie was climbing the pole on one end of the swing set. When he got to the top, he tried to stand up and balance on the bar.

"Get down here!" I called. "If you break your neck, I'm the one who'll get in trouble!"

"It's like a balance beam," said Sofi. "He can do it."

"We taught Butterscotch to jump the hurdle!" I told Sal as Ollie slid back down. "Come and see!"

So, we went back home and tried to get Butterscotch to jump over the hurdle again. The problem was, I didn't have any more dog treats, and when we told her to jump, she just stood there! Ollie said we were probably just making it up.

Ollie and Sofi climbed up to the treehouse platform, and Ollie swung on the rope to try to catch the bar. He almost made it. Sofi tried it next. She grabbed the bar, swung back and forth a few times, then jumped to the ground and stuck her landing on the first try. She's used to flying around in the air in gymnastics. Ollie's nose was so out of joint, I couldn't help laughing.

"Do you think we'll see Susie in the mirror tomorrow?" asked Sal.

"I hope so," I said, "because tomorrow's the last day we'll be there. We have to go to the dentist on Thursday, and Friday I'm going on a sleepover with Mady and Taylor."

"I hope so, too," he said, "because I've got an idea. You know the reports we have to write for history? I'm gonna ask Susie what it was like to be a slave kid, and write about it!"

All the fifth graders have to write a report on something about the Civil War. We were supposed to turn in our topics as soon as we got back from break. Dang! I wished I'd thought of that. "Good idea," I said.

"Yeah, I'll take my notebook with me tomorrow, and write down everything she tells us," he said.

"And I still want to draw a picture of her," I said.

"YAAAAAY!" yelled Ollie. He finally managed to catch the trapeze bar as he swung from the rope. He dropped to the ground and gave a bow. "Tell me about this underground railroad," he said. "Is it like in a tunnel?"

"No, it's not even a railroad at all," said Sal. "It's what they called this secret system to help slaves escape. You know about slaves, right?"

Ollie nodded, but Sofi said, "No."

"It's when you own another person, and you can

make them do whatever you want. Some white people here in America owned Black people, like Susie, and made them work on their farms," I explained.

"But how can you own a person?" asked Sofi. "Did they buy them at the store?"

"I think they just captured them and, like, kidnapped them," said Sal, "but anyway, after they got them here, then their kids became slaves, too, and they couldn't get away."

"And sometimes the owners were mean to them, and beat them and stuff," I added.

Sofi looked frightened. "I don't want anybody to beat Susie!" she said.

"But they don't have slaves anymore," said Sal. "It's like we told Susie, there was a war a long time ago, and the slaves got freed.

"So anyway," he went on, "some people wanted to help the slaves get away from their owners, so they hid them in safe places where the owners couldn't find them, and that's what they mean by the underground railroad."

"But how did she wind up in Granny's house? Is it a safe place?" asked Ollie.

"I guess so," I said. "You know, we should find out if the underground railroad came here. Maybe we could ask Wally and Betty." Wally and Betty Howard are our next-door neighbors. They're old like Grandma and Grandpa, and they've lived in the same house forever, so they know everything that's happened around here. They're pretty special to us because they took us to the Indian cemetery where Samuel Grayhawk found his sister. We ran next door.

Betty answered the door when we rang the bell and invited us in. "Is this your new look for spring?" she asked when she saw my hair. "You look like one of the flowers! How about a cookie?"

"Yesssss!" said Ollie, and Betty gave us each a chocolate chip cookie as Wally came into the kitchen. We didn't tell her we'd just eaten a bunch of biscotti.

"Well, hello! I thought we might see you this week. Aren't you on spring break?" He looked at my hair and grinned, but didn't say anything.

"Wally," I said, "you know we're studying history this year, and we've learned about the Civil War and slavery. Could you help us find out more about the underground railroad?"

"Like if any slaves escaped around here," said Sal.

"Well, OK," said Wally, as he turned on his computer. "Let's see what we can find out."

"So, you know it wasn't a real railroad," said Betty. We all nodded.

"And you probably know that most of the slaves were in the southern states," said Wally. "Big farms and plantations, where they grew cotton and sugar, needed lots of workers to plant and harvest the crops. The farmers tried to use Indians as slaves at first, but they just slipped away, so back in the 1600s they started bringing Africans over to America to work on the plantations."

"And some slave owners were very cruel," said Betty. "The slaves did all the hard work, they didn't get paid, and they lived in poor, run-down shacks. Owners could even buy and sell slaves, like they were a horse or a cow."

"Huh, I'd just run away if I was a slave!" said Ollie. "I wouldn't let anybody do that to me!"

"It wasn't easy to escape," said Betty. "If a runaway got caught, he would be sent back to his owner. He'd probably be punished for running away."

"So how did any slaves get away, then?" asked Ollie.

Wally found another website that explained it more. "Here it says slaves usually just ran away at night and stayed hidden until they got to the north," he read. "There were certain places, called stations, where people would hide them and give them food once they got there. It was very dangerous, and they never knew who they could trust."

"You know there was a station of the underground railroad not far from here, don't you?" said Betty.

My jaw dropped. "No!"

Susie's story was beginning to make sense!

Chapter 9

Ghost Town: Quindaro

"**A**n underground railroad station near here?" asked Sal. "Where?"

"At Quindaro. That was an old settlement along the Missouri River before the Civil War."

"Quindaro?" asked Ollie. "I never heard of it!"

"It's not really a town anymore," said Wally. "It's part of Kansas City, Kansas, up by where the Kansas and Missouri Rivers come together—not far from that Indian cemetery where we took you kids."

"Is the station still there?" asked Ollie. "Can we go see it?"

"It wasn't a regular train station. That's just what they called places where runaways could stop for help. It might be in someone's house, or maybe a barn or shed.

Only a few people who were in on the secret knew where they were," said Wally.

"All the buildings in old Quindaro are gone now," said Betty. "You can't tell there was ever a town there."

"So it's a *ghost* town!" I said. *And a good place for a ghost to live*, I thought.

Wally clicked on another website and read for a minute. "It says here Quindaro was a pretty active stop on the underground railroad," he said. "Abolitionists—that's the people who were against slavery—helped set up the town and worked to get runaway slaves to freedom."

"Did any slaves come to Quindaro on the underground railroad from Missouri?" asked Ollie.

"Probably," said Betty. "Missouri was a border state, so there were slave owners there. Kansas would have been the closest free territory, so I'm sure some of the slaves who escaped came from there."

"There's no way to know for sure, though," said Wally. "They didn't keep any records. It was too dangerous to write things down. It was against the law to help slaves escape, and if a white person was caught helping them, he could be arrested and sent to prison."

Sal looked shocked. "Are you serious?" he asked. "It was against the law?"

"Well, as hard as it is to believe," said Betty, "slavery was legal in the southern states. There were real battles along the border between slaveholders in Missouri and free-staters in Kansas. That's why they called the area 'Bleeding Kansas.'"

"That's terrible!" I said. "You mean people actually got killed trying to help the slaves? It doesn't talk about that in our history book!"

"So I guess if someone did escape on the underground railroad, they'd want to keep it a secret," said Sal. "It sounds pretty dangerous."

"Exactly," said Betty.

We thanked Wally and Betty for their help (and the cookies) and started back to our house. On the way, I said, "Now I really have to talk to Granny Bets! I have to find out if she knows about Susie in the attic *and* what she knows about Quindaro."

"What are you waiting for?" asked Sal. "Your grandma said you should visit her."

"I know," I said. "The problem is how can we talk to her with nobody listening in?"

We headed for our back yard. "Guys," I said, "I'm still wracking my brain trying to figure out why Susie doesn't have a body! And if she doesn't have one, what is it we see in the mirror?"

"Well," said Sal, "Samuel's the only ghost we knew before this, so we don't really know what's normal."

"Uh, like any of this is normal?" I asked.

"So?" said Ollie. "It's not like they have rules or something, is it?"

"We can figure it out," said Sal. "Think...how are Samuel and Susie the same, and how are they different?"

"They both died when they were kids, and they knew they were dead," I said, counting off on my fingers.

"And they were both trying to find somebody... Samuel was looking for his sister, and Susie's waiting for her dad," said Sal.

"Oh, right!" I said. "And Samuel couldn't go on to the spirit world until he found her! Do you think if Susie finds out what happened to her dad, she can go...back to her grave?"

"But Susie can't make her body come back," said Ollie.

"Maybe she doesn't have enough strength," said Sal. "Remember, Samuel said it took lots of strength to make it so we could see him."

"Maybe it's because she had the measles," said Sofi.

"Why would that...oh, I get it!" I said. "Susie was so sick before she died...maybe she's too weak to bring her body back."

"But she had enough strength to pick up the doll and shut the chest lid," said Ollie. "And she picked up the Monopoly game."

"What else could it be?" said Sal. "Susie was buried with her mom and sister—"

"That's it!" I cried. "Susie was buried! That's the big difference between her and Samuel! Samuel died in the cellar and nobody ever found him, so he never got put in a grave—and his body just went wherever his ghost was!"

"Oh, right!" said Sal. "And Susie *was* buried, so her body's in her grave. She said she's just a shadow of what she used to be..."

"And that's what we see! Only it's not her shadow, it's her reflection in the mirror!" I finished.

"Yeah, her reflection...her ghost shows up as her reflection," said Sal.

"But she goes around the room and does things, even if we can't see her doing it," said Ollie.

"Yeah, she nearly amputated my fingers," said Sal.

"But that was before she talked to us," I said. "Don't you see? Yesterday it was just Ollie and me, and she was trying to talk to us, but we had to leave."

"And when we came back, you were with us," said Ollie.

"Oh, yeah...when she saw Sofi and me, she was afraid we were slave owners' kids," said Sal. "She didn't trust us."

"And she didn't want us to take the doll," said Sofi.

"Yeah, the doll must be pretty special to Susie, or she wouldn't have grabbed it away," said Ollie. "Maybe it's magic, and it helps her show up in the mirror."

"Duh," I said. "There's no such thing as magic!"

"Uh, most people don't think there's such a thing as ghosts," said Sal. "Ollie might be on to something."

Chapter 10
A Lesson on Slavery

The next morning Sal brought a notebook and pen so he could write down everything Susie told us about her life as a slave. I reminded myself to start on a picture of her. I'd been so wrapped up in listening to her yesterday, I hadn't even thought of drawing.

On the way to Granny's house, I asked Grandpa Louie if he'd ever heard of Quindaro.

"Sure," he said. "The old grounds aren't far from the house."

"Have you been there?" asked Sal.

"I have, but there's nothing to see," said Grandpa. "All the buildings fell down years ago."

When we got to Granny's house, Coco was waiting for us on the porch. Grandma had brought a small bag of cat food, so we took Coco inside and poured some into a bowl. Sofi got a paper towel and cleaned up her muddy paws.

After Coco ate, we helped Grandma and Grandpa clean out the pantry. When Grandma said we could go play, we all stomped up to the attic as fast as we could and gathered in front of the mirror.

"Susie?" I called. "Can you come out and see us?" I had my sketch pad and pencil ready.

We didn't have to wait long. I felt the usual cold air around us, and saw Susie appear in the mirror, standing behind us like she always did.

"Don't you want to sit down here with us?" asked Sal. He scooted over a little to make some room for her, which was pretty weird because she wasn't really behind us. Susie gave him a funny look, but after a minute, she knelt down behind us...that's what it looked like in the mirror, anyway.

"Susie, we want to be your friends," I said. "So why did you try to scare us?"

"Did you straighten up the game board yesterday?" asked Sal as he pointed to the Monopoly board, which was still on the floor where we'd left it.

Susie dipped her head. "I'm used to pickin' up after young'uns," she said.

"And did you grab the doll out of my hand, and shut the chest lid when Sal tried to pick it up?" I asked.

Susie looked down. "That doll, it's all I got left of my family...I lost my mama and daddy, my brothers and sisters...the doll helps me remember 'em. Can't lose that too. Never meant to scare y'all."

"Don't worry," said Sofi. "We won't take your doll."

"So your mom had a baby after you ran away?" asked Sal. "That was your sister Rebecca?"

"She born in the winter after we got here," said Susie.

"You sang her that song!" said Ollie. "The 'hush-a-bye' song for the baby!"

Susie nodded. "Mama sung that to all her babies."

"Susie," I said, "do you remember the name of the town where you lived with Mr. and Mrs. Armstrong?"

"That'd be Quindaro," said Susie. "I hear other folks what runned away from their owners come there."

"I knew it!" I said, and gave Sal a high five. "So, why are you in our Granny's house? I mean, this isn't Quindaro, so how did you end up here?"

She looked around at the room. "I stayed in the old room at Miz Armstrong's house, till she move out and come to the new place. I just come with her."

"You mean *this* is her *new* house?" I asked. Susie nodded. I almost laughed—Granny's house is the oldest house I've ever seen!

"Wait, you mean Mrs. Armstrong knew you were still there?" asked Sal. "After you died?

Susie thought for a minute. "After I died...after we

was buried...I knowed I had to come back...to wait for my daddy," she said. "So when I come back, I see Miz Armstrong just left our room the same. She felt awful bad about us dyin' before he come. Figured she want me to have a place to wait."

"But Mrs. Armstrong's been gone for years!" I said.

"I figure she tell whoever live here to leave our room be," said Susie. "Don't know what she tell 'em, but nobody ever bother me."

"Susie, your story is just...out of this world! I want to hear what it was like to be a slave, and how you escaped, then I'm gonna write a report about it," said Sal.

"Story?" said Susie. "I ain't tellin' no story."

"Sure you are!" I said. "Your life is a story!"

"Do you know when you were born?" asked Sal.

"No, sir, not sure," said Susie.

Sal giggled. "You don't have to call me 'sir,'" he said. "So how old were you when you, uh, died?"

"Just turned twelve," said Susie. "My baby sister, she's three."

"OK," said Sal, "if you knew about the war, but not about the slaves getting set free, you must have been born about...1850." *There he goes again*, I thought. "And you were born in Missouri?" he asked.

"Born on Mr. Chase's farm. He own my mama, and me, and my two sisters and three brothers," Susie answered.

"And your dad lived on another farm?" I asked. "He didn't even live with you?"

"He live with Mr. Briggs," said Susie. "He come to visit us on Wednesday and Sunday."

"Well," said Ollie, "my friend Matthew's dad doesn't live with him, and only sees him on weekends."

"Yeah, but nobody *owns* him!" I said.

"So what was it really like to be a slave?" asked Sal.

"You don't *know*?" she stared at him.

"Hey, I get that you didn't want to be sold, and you had to work for the white people, but what did you have to do?" he asked. "You lived on a farm, and all, but how hard was it, really?"

Well, I thought sparks were gonna shoot out of Susie's eyes! Nobody else said anything, and I know Sal was sort of embarrassed because he stammered and said, "I mean, I don't know what you had to do. Did you pick cotton or what?"

"Slaves do all the work," said Susie, "whatever Mr. or Miz Chase tell us to do. In the house, cook, wash, clean, sew the clothes, churn the butter. In the garden, hoe the dirt, plant the seeds, pick the corn and dig the taters. In the fields, plant the corn and wheat and tobacco, cut and tie the tobacco. Feed the animals, milk the cows, shoe the hosses. Kill the chickens, butcher the hogs, smoke the meat. Everything."

Wow, I guess she told him!

"*You* did all *that*?" asked Ollie. "But you were, like, just a kid!"

"Not all that," said Susie. "I was a house slave. Still had plenty to do. Mama was learnin' me to sew the clothes for the master and missus."

"Mr. and Mrs. Chase?" asked Sal. He was writing as fast as he could.

Susie nodded. "Miz Chase say I got a good hand with the needle. She want me to make dresses for her daughters, and shirts and britches for her boys."

"And you're only twelve? That's pretty awesome!" I said.

"Did they make you eat bread and water?" asked Ollie. "You look so skinny!"

"Never went hungry," Susie said. "Mr. Chase got lots of animals, cows, pigs, chickens, ducks, geese, turkeys. 'Course we had to do all the work fixin' food for the Chases and for us. Men and boys did the butcherin' and hang the meat in the smokehouse. Mama and us girls, we pluck and dress the chickens and geese, and save the feathers for the beds. Except we didn't get no feathers for our beds, Mr. Chase's family got 'em all.

"And we grew corn and taters, beans and turnips. We made cornmeal for cornbread, and Mr. Chase give us some wheat flour sometimes. My mama made the best biscuits! And we can pick all the dandelions we want, and cook up the greens all summer."

"You ate dandelions?!" said Ollie. "Yuck!"

"Don't be rude!" I said. I whacked the back of his head and he punched me in the arm. I have to admit, though, eating dandelions sounded pretty terrible.

"What about cookies or cake?" asked Sal.

"Mr. Chase got a lot of fruit trees, so we had apples and peaches for pies, and jam and jelly for the biscuits… and maple syrup. And whenever Mr. Briggs give Daddy some molasses, Mama made tea cakes and gingerbread!"

Right then I heard a voice from the second-floor landing. Grandpa Louie was calling us. "You kids ready for lunch?"

"Oh, no!" said Ollie. "I don't want to leave now!"

"Me neither," said Sal. "We need to think of an excuse to stay here."

"Right," I said. "Susie, we have to go for a while, but we'll come back as soon as we can."

All this time I had been sketching, trying to get a good drawing of Susie on paper as she talked. I held my sketch pad up to the mirror so she could see. It wasn't perfect, but you could tell who it was supposed to be.

Susie put her hand to her heart. "Oh, my goodness!" she said. "You make a picture of *me*? Ain't nobody ever done that before!"

She liked it! I propped the sketch pad against the mirror and we all hurried down the stairs.

Chapter 11
Growing Up a Slave

When we got downstairs, Grandpa Louie said he needed to make a run to the donation center, so we carried boxes and bags to the van. Once it was all loaded, there wasn't room for all six of us, so Grandma said she would stay with us kids while Grandpa took the van to the donation center.

"We can stay by ourselves," I told Grandma Libby. "We won't bother anything, and we'll stay inside until you get back."

"I don't know…," said Grandma.

"It'll be fine!" I said. "You know, now that I'm eleven, Mom and Dad said I could start babysitting, and Sal stays with Sofi all the time when their mom's at work. We can take care of Sofi and Ollie—we're very responsible!"

"Well, I guess it'll be OK," said Grandma. "We'll pick up something for lunch and bring it back with us." We waved to them from the front door.

"You're not babysitting me!" cried Ollie as soon as Grandma went out the door.

"You got that right!" I said. "If I was, you'd be in time out the rest of your life!" I was already on my way to the stairs. "Hey, we got lucky! Come on, we can stay in the attic until they get back!"

We all ran up the stairs and sat down in front of the mirror. Of course, we couldn't resist making silly faces, just for the fun of it, so we were taken by surprise when we heard singing.

"SHHH!" I said, and stopped short. I put my finger to my lips and we listened.

"That's Susie singing!" whispered Ollie. Then the singing stopped, the air turned cold, and Susie was suddenly there.

"We heard you singing again," I said. "What was that song?"

"'Wade in the water,'" said Susie. "It's a song about hidin' from the patrollers chasin' us. You gotta get in the water so's the dogs can't smell you."

"Whoa!" said Ollie. Sofi looked horrified.

"Oh, my God!" I said. "They actually hunted you down with dogs?"

Susie nodded. "They do anything they can to catch slaves what escaped."

"Well, I'm glad they didn't catch you," said Ollie.

"You were telling us that even kids…children…like you had to do lots of work," said Sal. He was ready to get more for his report.

"I start cleanin' the wool at four years old, gettin' it ready to spin into yarn," said Susie. "We was about never too young to work for the master."

"What else did little girls do?" asked Sofi.

"Lots," said Susie. "Little bitty ones pick up firewood and pull weeds in the garden. By five or six they feed the chickens. Gather the eggs, and better not break one!"

"What about the boys?" asked Ollie.

"Start young, helpin' with the animals. Then they go into the tobacco fields, cuttin' and tyin' and hangin'. Clean and fix the wagons and tools. Boys my age was doin' a man's work," she said. "My biggest brother, he learned to ride a hoss and drive a wagon with a team. Them boys, they was always wore out."

"Jeez!" said Sal. "I wouldn't know how to do any of that stuff!"

"But your job doesn't sound so hard," said Ollie. "You got to stay inside and make clothes."

"Do you think you could make your own clothes?" I asked him.

"I don't mind the stitchin' so much," said Susie, "but lots of other work come before that. If it's wool dresses or britches they want, we got to shear the sheep, and card the wool, and spin the yarn. Then we got to thread the loom and weave the cloth. Cotton dresses is better, 'cause Miz Chase gets the bolts of calico for us."

"Calico?" said Sofi, hugging Coco to her. "You made dresses out of cat fur?"

"Like this," said Susie, pointing to her skirt. It was faded blue, but we could see a pattern of some kind in yellow and red.

"I think it means cloth with lots of colors," I said.

"Makin' the clothes was a chore," said Susie. "I got cricks in my shoulders from leanin' over the stitchin', and fingers all bloody from the needles. And makin' soap was stinky and hot. But it wasn't as bad as workin' in the barn. My brother got kicked in the head by a hoss and he never could see out of one eye again."

We all just looked at her in horror.

"All that work!" Sal said finally. "And you never got paid for anything?"

"Mama never get no money," said Susie. "Only time we ever have money's if we catch some fish to sell. But money can't buy us freedom."

I was trying to imagine a life like that, when we

heard Grandma calling up the stairs. "Kids? We're back! We brought tacos for lunch!"

I hadn't even heard the van pulling onto the gravel driveway. It's a good thing Grandma didn't hear Susie talking!

"Susie, we have to go again for a while. We'll come back, though," I promised.

Susie looked up from beneath her long lashes. "Been so long since I talked to anybody…not since Miz Armstrong."

We all scrambled out of the attic and down the stairs.

Sofi shared bits of her taco with Coco, who liked the meat and cheese, but the tomatoes and lettuce, not so much.

"Why do you like the attic so much?" asked Grandpa as we ate.

"It's like a secret little playhouse," I said.

"And it's cool to be up so high, and look down at everything from the window," said Ollie.

"Hard to believe you're having fun in a place with no Wi-Fi," said Grandpa.

Grandma said we would start clearing out the upstairs bedrooms after lunch. She said most of the inside work would be done this week, and by the time the flowers started to bloom, the house would be ready to sell.

"I wonder who will buy it?" said Sal.

"It's over 100 years old," said Grandpa Louie. "It wouldn't surprise me if somebody tears it down and builds something new."

"But they can't tear it down!" said Ollie. "What about…?" I kicked him under the table.

"Why not?" said Grandpa. "Whoever buys it can do whatever they want with it."

"What will happen to the stuff in the attic?" I asked Grandpa. "Are you gonna take it to Granny?"

"I haven't even gone up there to look," he said. "Granny says there's just some old things that were here when she moved in, they're not even hers. I guess I ought to see if there's anything we can donate, or if we should just throw it all away."

I didn't say anything, but Ollie looked at me with wide eyes. What would happen to Susie if her stuff got taken away? And what if the house got torn down? I sat there stunned as Grandpa started toward the attic stairs. Sal grabbed my arm. "Your sketch pad," he whispered.

Uh-oh!

"We'll go too!" I cried.

Chapter 12
Susie's Sampler

We all ran ahead of Grandpa, trying to get to the attic before he did. The Monopoly game was still on the rug, and my sketch pad sat propped by the mirror where I had left it. I quickly turned to a new sheet on the pad, just as Grandpa caught up with us. Otherwise, the attic room looked just like it had the first time we saw it.

Grandpa's so tall, he had to stoop over so he wouldn't bump his head on the ceiling. He took a quick look and said, "Not much up here worth keeping."

"Granny might want it," said Ollie.

"Trust me, she doesn't," said Grandpa, and he turned toward the stairs.

"Why don't you just leave it?" I asked. "If it was here when Granny moved in, maybe somebody else could use it."

"Not likely," said Grandpa. "That chair's not safe to sit in, and the mirror's a piece of junk."

"When are you going to take it away?" I asked.

"It can wait till everything else is done," said Grandpa. "I'm getting out of here before I knock myself out on the ceiling beams."

"Come on, we better help clean up some before we come back up," I said. I started to follow Grandpa, and Sal came with me.

"I want to stay here and play!" said Ollie. "I'm tired of cleaning up!"

"Don't be a brat! You can't stay and play if I have to go help Grandpa," I said. "It's not fair!"

"Get over it," said Sal, rolling his eyes. "Can't you just cut him a little slack? Let him stay up here with Sofi." Ollie gets away with everything, but I decided it wasn't worth arguing about.

"We're not coming back any more after today, are we?" asked Sal.

"We have to go to the dentist tomorrow, and do some other stuff," I said. "So this might be the last time we ever get to talk to Susie."

"I wish we had more time with her, like we had with Samuel!" he said.

"You mean we'll never come to see Coco again?" asked Sofi.

"Probably not," I said. Sofi looked heartbroken.

"Come on, they don't help much, anyway," said Sal.

The two of us went downstairs and emptied out a couple of old dressers. I was still miffed that Ollie got to stay in the attic, so I hurried to get it all done. As we went back to the attic, I whispered to Sal, "Finally! I wonder if Susie came out to see Ollie and Sofi?"

When we got there, Ollie was on the floor with his Legos and Sofi was holding Susie's doll and playing with Coco. I hurried over to look into the mirror, and saw that Susie was kneeling on the floor beside them.

"What have you been doing all this time?" I asked.

"Oh, just playing," said Ollie.

"Susie sang us some songs," said Sofi. "We're having fun."

"Been a long time since I had young'uns to look after," Susie said. Ollie and Sofi both grinned, like they were loving it. "Puts me in mind of my little brother and sister."

"You can have Ollie if you want him," I said. "How come you let Sofi hold your doll? I thought you didn't want us touching it."

"She ain't hurtin' it," said Susie. "She just playin.'"

Her face looked so soft when she looked at Ollie and Sofi, I was sorry I'd said anything about it. Susie hadn't had very much fun in her life.

I looked over and saw that the humpback chest was

open. Inside there was a folded piece of cloth, some colored thread, a silver thimble and some needles stuck in a piece of paper.

"Is this what you brought with you from Mr. Chase's when you ran away?" I asked.

"We didn't bring nothin," said Susie. "Just some food and the clothes we was wearin'. Miz Armstrong give Mama this chest and some sewin' things, and we made dresses and aprons for her."

I picked up the folded piece of cloth. It was a picture made with colored stitches. I held it up so that everybody could see it.

"What is it?" asked Ollie.

"Look at the names!" I said. In blue letters at the top of the cloth were the names "Birdie" and "Ezekiel." There were also flowers stitched beneath the names in red, yellow, pink and purple.

"My sampler," said Susie.

"Sampler?" asked Sal.

"Oh, I know!" I said. "It's what girls used to make to practice their sewing. Wow, it's really pretty!"

"So who are Birdie and E..ze..k…?" asked Ollie.

"Ezekiel," said Susie. "That be my mama and daddy. Miz Armstrong drawed the letters out for me, and I done the stitchin' while we was waitin' for my daddy."

I laid the sampler back inside the humpback chest.

"Susie told us she lived in a log cabin," said Ollie.

"Really?" said Sal. He got ready to write.

"Sure enough," said Susie. "All of us, mama, brothers, sisters, and the other slaves. Got two rooms and a big fireplace made out of stones from the field. Mama did all the cookin' there in that fireplace."

I almost shuddered at the thought of living in one room with Mom, Dad, and Ollie.

"Weren't much nice about that cabin," said Susie,

"'cept it keeped out the rain. No glass in the windows, like in Mr. Chase's big house. No planks on the floor, only dirt packed down hard. No chairs, just a table and a bench. And it was dark inside."

"Wasn't it cold in the winter?" I asked.

"Sure was. Mama and me, we make rugs out of the dress-makin' scraps to try and keep the floor warm," said Susie.

"Like that one?" I asked, pointing to one of the rugs on the attic floor.

Susie nodded. "Mama made that one before she died."

"You said Mr. and Mrs. Chase got to use all the feathers for their beds," said Sal. "What did you sleep on?"

"Sacks full of straw, on the floor," she said.

"So how many slaves were there at Mr. Chase's farm?" asked Sal. He was getting lots of good information for his report.

"'Bout twelve," said Susie. "Mr. Chase planted lots of tobacco, and he needed more help in the barns. That's why he selled my little brothers down to Arkansas. He got enough money to buy a bigger boy to work tobacco. Mama knowed I was good at stitchin' and she feared Mr. Chase could sell me for enough money to buy another boy."

"Was Mr. Chase mean to you?" asked Ollie.

"Did he beat you?" asked Sofi, looking frightened.

"He never pay me much mind," said Susie. "But Miz Chase, she complain about everything I do. I sew a nice straight seam, she makes me tear it out and do again. She say I move too slow when she call me. She say I eat too much. She don't like nothin' I do."

"*You* eat too much?" said Sal, laughing.

"She sounds like a witch," I said.

"I bet you hated Mr. and Mrs. Chase," said Ollie.

"Hate?" asked Susie. She thought for a moment. "Mr. Chase, he just a slave master. Better'n some I heared about. Now Miz Chase, I don't like her much, but don't reckon I hates her. My daddy told me it don't do no good to hate. Hatin' don't change nothin'. He just want me to get away, not get selled down to Arkansas or nowhere."

"Did you ever see your brothers again, after they got sold?" asked Ollie.

"Never seen 'em again. Broke Mama's heart. She so scared he gonna sell more of her babies, 'cause every year at New Year, it's slave-sellin' day. We got to go 'fore then. Me and Mama goes out after sundown one day and start walkin' and keep on goin' till we got to Kansas."

"How long did that take?" asked Sal.

"We walk at night and rest in the day," said Susie. "After about three days, a farm lady found us hidin' by the river. I near died of fright, but she telled Mama she won't turn us in."

Sal whistled. "You walked for three nights in the dark? That's pretty amazing."

"But when did you get on the railroad?" asked Ollie.

"Lady at the farm say we in Kansas Territory, free territory," said Susie. "She say she can't keep us at her place, 'cause raiders come sometimes, but she can help us get to the station."

"Raiders?" asked Ollie.

"Remember what Wally told us about Bleeding Kansas?" I said. "The slave owners sent people to go to houses along the border and see if they were hiding runaway slaves."

"So the lady was on the railroad!" said Sal.

"Lady's husband, he take us to Mr. and Miz Armstrong. They's Indians," she said. "Mama and me cooked and helped Miz Armstrong around the house, but didn't never go outside. Gotta stay hidin'. Just before Christmas, Mama borned my baby sister, Rebecca."

"But why did you have to hide, after you got to Kansas?" asked Sal. "Weren't you safe then?"

"Raiders is everywhere," said Susie. "They drag you back to your master if they catches you. Mr. and Miz Armstrong, they keep us hid in the house."

"Your life sounds terrible!" said Ollie. "How could you ever be happy?"

Susie looked thoughtful. "Lots of bad things happen," she said, "but lots of good things, too. I was happy to be alive and have my family. And my mama and daddy love me...."

"And you got away!" said Ollie. "Wasn't it a lot better once you got to Kansas?"

"Some ways," she said. "Lots of ways it's better, but my family got broke up..."

Susie's story was so sad, I wanted to do something to make her feel better. "Guys," I said, "let's do something fun with Susie!"

Chapter 13
Farewell to Susie and Coco?

"What *did* you do for fun?" Ollie asked Susie. "Did you have any toys? Did you play games?"

"Mama made dolls for us," said Susie. "Made 'em out of scraps from our dresses, and she stitched pretty faces on 'em. Like Rebecca's doll. And she filled little sacks with dry beans for my brothers to throw. We play hoss shoes, and Miz Chase's boys showed us how to play checkers. We make the checkers out of wood, or use rocks. We'd climb trees, and go fishin' in the creek, and catch frogs. When it got real hot, we'd go wadin'."

"Like the song you sang," said Ollie.

"And I had me a cat. Named him Midnight, 'cause he was all black 'cept for a white spot between his eyes. Had to leave him behind when I runned away."

"Oh, Susie, I'm so sorry," I said. I was trying to think of a game we could play with her, but what kind of game can you do with somebody who's only a reflection in a mirror? "We could have a spelling bee," I said.

"Oh, right!" said Sal. "You know how to spell, don't you, Susie?"

Susie gave him a blank look. "Spell?" she asked.

Uh-oh, I thought. "Susie, do you know how to read?"

"Mr. and Miz Chase, they don't let us learn how to read! Say we don't need to know how. But they did learn us our numbers, so's we can count," said Susie.

"I know!" said Ollie. "Twenty questions!"

"Good idea!" said Sal. "Anybody can do that! OK, Susie, think of something...don't tell us what...and we'll guess what it is. We get twenty tries."

Susie didn't say anything, and I wasn't sure she understood, so I said, "It can be an animal, or a thing, like the chair or something, OK? Are you ready?" She nodded.

"Is it an animal?" asked Sofi. She nodded again.

"Is it a cat?" asked Ollie. Susie shook her head. This seemed to be working.

Hmmm, I thought, *Susie lived on a farm...* "Does it live in the barn?" I asked. No.

Ollie asked if it was a wild animal. Yes. Four questions, sixteen to go.

"Does it eat other animals?" asked Sal. No. Five

questions. Everybody started shouting questions: Does it fly? No. Does it make nests? Yes. Does it live in the forest? Yes. Can it run fast? Yes. Is it a deer? No. A fox? No. Can it climb trees? Yes. Is it a bear? No.

"I know!" cried Ollie. "Is it a squirrel?"

Susie broke into a big smile. "It's a squirrel," she said. She was actually laughing!

"Good job!" said Sal. "Now it's your turn, Ollie. Remember, you can't make it an airplane or something Susie never heard of."

After the game, Susie seemed just like one of us. It was great to see her laughing and having fun.

"You look happy, Susie," said Sofi.

"Ain't felt this good since I was back at Mr. Chase's, with all the family," she said. "Sunday afternoons, we'd sing and dance till after dark. I love singin', and my daddy, he played a mouth-organ like to bring the house down!"

"What's a mouth-organ?" asked Ollie.

Susie held up her hands in front of her mouth, and moved them from side to side.

"A harmonica!" cried Sofi.

"Oh, my gosh," I said, looking at the others. "There was a harmonica in Granny's locker! How weird is that!"

"Wish I could've heared him play that mouth organ one more time," Susie said sadly. She wiped a tear from her cheek, but then she smiled, a really beautiful smile.

That's when I noticed that she had dimples in her cheeks, just like Ollie and me!

"Bein' here with y'all," she said, "it almost makes me forget my troubles...."

We were so wrapped up in listening to Susie, we jumped when we heard Grandma calling to us that it was time to leave.

"Oh, Susie," I said, "we have to go now...and I don't know if we'll ever be back again! I wish we could help you find out about your dad!"

"Y'all been a joy to me, havin' somebody to talk to," she said. "Make me feel like I got a family again."

"But you know they're gonna move your stuff, don't you?" said Sal. "They're gonna sell the house, and it might get torn down! What will do you then?" He sounded really worried.

Susie looked around the room. "Don't know," she said. "The things here, they's a comfort for me, but I don't reckon I needs 'em. Only thing's the doll. Hate to lose that."

"But where can you go?" asked Sofi.

"If you found out what happened to your dad, could you go back to your grave?" I asked. I couldn't stand the thought of Susie with nowhere to stay forever!

Grandma called again. "Come on, you kids, we're going to be late!"

"We have to go, Susie," I said. "I'm so sorry we

couldn't help you find out about your dad!"

"Thank you for telling us about your life," said Sal. "I hope you find somewhere safe to go!"

"I'll miss you, Susie," said Sofi.

"Me, too," said Ollie.

I never thought anything would be as hard as saying goodbye to Samuel that last time, but this was just as bad. Not only because we'd be losing Susie forever, but because we couldn't do anything to help her. As we gazed in the mirror, she did another little curtsy and faded away. The room warmed up, and we picked up our stuff and started down the stairs. I went last, looking around the room and into the mirror. The lump in my stomach was so heavy I was afraid I'd throw up.

I hardly remember loading the van and getting in for the drive home. All I could think about was what might happen to Susie when the house got sold. Where would she go? Who would help her find out about her dad?

I was only half-listening as Ollie gabbed on to Grandpa about the war medals. Nobody else had much to say, and Sofi seemed even quieter than usual. She had to be really upset at leaving Coco. I twisted around to look into the back seat of the van where she and Sal were sitting. *Hmmm, Sofi looks almost happy,* I thought...then I sucked in my breath. Before I could say anything, Sal put his finger to his lips. As Ollie chattered away, I saw a bit of black fur poking out from inside Sofi's jacket.

Chapter 14

Is Susie Doomed?

———————————————

"**W**hat will your mom say?" I asked Sofi as soon as Grandpa dropped us off at home. Sofi looked up at Sal.

"Dad'll be home first, and we'll tell him she was lost and needed a home," said Sal. "Mom won't be home from work until seven." He opened his backpack and took out the bag of cat food Grandma had brought to Granny's house. "I hope your grandma isn't too mad about us taking the food."

"You can bring her over to our back yard for now," said Ollie. "Let's go practice Ninja stuff!"

We went to our back yard to wait until Mr. Martelli got home. I went inside to get Butterscotch while Sofi put some cat food out on the porch. When Butterscotch saw her, she went and sniffed. Coco arched her back and hissed, and Butterscotch shrank back.

"It's OK, she won't hurt you," said Sofi, picking Coco up and petting her. Butterscotch sniffed her some more, then backed away.

"We'll never see Susie again, will we?" asked Sofi.

"I don't know," said Sal. "She's waiting for her dad to come, and he's probably been dead for 100 years! If she doesn't find out what happened to him, she could be waiting forever!" I could tell Sal was truly worried about her.

"And who knows what'll happen to her when they sell the house?" asked Ollie.

"Do you think if she found out what happened to him, she'd go back to her grave?" I asked. "She didn't get a chance to tell us."

"Well, he's the reason she came back," said Sal. "So if she finds out about him, she won't have any reason to stay. But how will she find out? And what if they tear down the house?"

"Or throw away the mirror?" asked Ollie.

"And the doll," said Sofi.

"I want to talk to Granny Bets right away," I said. "We need to find out how much she knows, but we have to be careful not to give Susie away!"

"Maybe Mom would take us to see her," said Ollie. "While Grandma and Grandpa are over at her house."

"Good idea," said Sal. "Hey, there's my dad. Come

on, Sofi, we better get him on our side before Mom gets home."

LATER, AT DINNER, Dad said, "It sounds like you two really got into helping Grandma and Grandpa at Granny's house. Did they pay you or something?"

"No!" I said. "We wouldn't ask them for money!" Actually, I wished I'd thought of it—Grandma and Grandpa always give us whatever we want.

"We found some awesome medals in Granny's locker," Ollie said. "My great-grandpa was a war hero! He even got shot!"

"I know," said Mom. "He had a scar on his arm from the bullet, but he never talked to me about it. I was still in school when he died."

"Grandpa said I should ask Granny about them. Do you think we could go visit her?"

"And could we take Sal and Sofi?" I asked. "There was a lot of stuff in Granny's trunk we want to know about."

"Honey, Granny's not very strong, and her health isn't as good as it was," said Mom. "I don't know if she's up to having four kids come over."

"But we just want to talk to her!" said Ollie. "I promise we'll be good!"

"Please!" I said. "Grandpa said himself that we should ask her about the medals. And she *is* getting old—what if she died and we never had another chance to talk to her?"

Mom looked at Dad, who just shrugged. "That makes sense," he said. "What could it hurt for an hour or so?" Mom gave in, and said we could visit Granny the next day. I ran to the hall to call Sal and tell him.

When I got up Thursday morning, I saw sunshine through the window—finally—and it hit me that spring break was more than half over! Mady and Taylor would both be back in town tomorrow, and we'd be sleeping over at Mady's Friday night. It hardly felt like I'd had a break at all—why did I have to find another ghost? I made up my mind to have fun the last few days of break, and try not to worry every minute about Susie.

After our visit to the dentist that morning, we went to the back yard. I practiced getting Butterscotch to jump the hurdle while Ollie worked on swinging from the rope to the trapeze bar. Butterscotch wasn't trying very hard, so we decided to take her for a walk. When we came around to the front of the house, we saw Sofi on her front step with Coco, and went over to say hello.

"What did your mom say about Coco?" asked Ollie.

"Umm, she was a little mad," said Sofi, "but my birthday's coming soon, and she said if I take good care of her, I can keep her! We went out last night and got her a new bed, and some food and toys, and some cat litter, and Mom showed me how to fix up her litter box." *Wow, I thought, that's the most words I've ever heard Sofi say!*

"Eeuuw!" said Ollie.

"It's OK," said Sofi, "'cause I love her!"

Sal must have heard us talking, because he came out the front door with a baseball and glove. "How about a little practice, Ollie?" he asked.

"Let me get my glove!" he yelled, and ran across the street to our house.

While we waited for him, Sal asked, "Aren't you worried about Susie? What's going to happen to her if the house gets torn down?"

"I don't know," I said with a sigh. "I just don't understand about where Susie really *is*. Does she come from her grave to the mirror?"

Sal shrugged. "Do you think your granny might be able to help?"

"I've been thinking about how we're going to talk to her about Susie without sounding insane," I said as Ollie came running across the street with his glove. "So, are you ready to write your report about slavery?"

"Yeah, I think so. I'm gonna use almost everything Susie told us…but I've been thinking, remember how she told us the lady who helped her was an Indian, and lots of Indians lived in Quindaro? I wonder if they were Wyandots? You know, like Samuel?"

"What was their name again?" I asked. "Armstrong or something like that?"

"Yeah, and that name seems so familiar..." said Sal.

"We could ask Wally and Betty if many Wyandots lived in Quindaro," I said. "Let's go right now and see them before you go practice! Sofi, you can bring Coco to meet them."

Chapter 15
A Connection with Samuel

So, the four of us took Butterscotch and Coco and rang the Howards' doorbell. Betty let us in.

"Is there a new member of the Martelli family?" she asked when she saw Coco.

"This is Coco," said Sofi. "She's a calico cat!"

"She certainly is," said Wally as he came to the front hall. "What are you all up to today? Baseball?"

"Yeah, break's almost over so we gotta have as much fun as we can!" said Ollie.

"Right," I said. "But Sal and I have to write a report for school when we go back, and we have a question. Remember how you helped us look up the underground railroad, and you told us about Quindaro? That's what I'm gonna write about, and then I heard that some

Indians lived in Quindaro. Is that true?"

Wally opened the top of his computer and started a new page. "There were Indians from several tribes living in the area, and I think some of them are still there. You know they have that casino up by the cemetery where we took you kids." He typed some things on his keyboard and then clicked on an entry.

"Quindaro," he said. "Here's a good note. The town was named after a woman named Nancy Quindaro Brown, who was a Wyandot Indian. Isn't your friend a Wyandot?"

"Yes!" we all said excitedly. "Samuel was—I mean he is—a Wyandot!"

"And it says Quindaro is a Wyandot word that means, roughly, 'bundle of sticks,'" said Wally.

"Huh?" said Ollie. "Why would they name it that?"

"It's a good name for a community," said Betty, reading from the computer screen. "It suggests strength in numbers. A bundle of sticks is stronger than just one stick, and a group of people, in a town, are stronger than just one person."

"The Wyandots must have been important in Quindaro if they named the town after one of them," said Wally.

"Do you think Indian families would have helped slaves who escaped on the underground railroad?" I asked.

"Yeah!" said Ollie. "Did the Indians and the slaves who escaped stick together, like a bundle of sticks?"

"Probably," said Wally. "Remember, the Indians knew how it felt to be treated badly, and I'm sure some of them tried to help."

"My report's going to be about what life was like for slave kids," said Sal. "But I don't understand some of the things I've heard about it."

"Like what?" asked Wally.

"Well, why didn't the slave owners want them to learn to read and write?" asked Sal. "What was so bad about that?"

"You've probably heard the saying, 'knowledge is power,'" said Betty. "Think about it—if slaves could read, they would know that there was a movement to abolish slavery. The owners wanted to keep them from finding out about efforts to free them."

"And slave owners were terrified of a slave rebellion," said Wally. "They didn't want the slaves communicating with each other and planning to overthrow their masters."

"If they could write," said Betty, "they could do things to trick their masters. You know, back then, written communication was all done by hand. If a slave knew how, he could write up a paper saying he'd been set free, and sign his master's name."

"Yeah, I see what you mean," said Sal. "And is it true

that even in Kansas, runaway slaves could be captured? I thought Kansas was a free state."

"Well," said Betty, "before the Civil War, Kansas wasn't a state at all—just a territory, and there were terrible fights over whether it would be a slave state or a free state."

"Oh, yeah, Bleeding Kansas!" said Ollie.

"And don't forget that law against helping slaves escape," said Wally. "It allowed patrollers to hunt down runaway slaves and return them to their masters—even in free states. They got a reward for returning slaves to their owners, and I expect they focused on Kansas because it's close to Missouri."

"So running away really *was* dangerous," said Sal. "Anybody who actually made it had to be pretty brave."

"And pretty lucky," said Wally.

We thanked Betty and Wally for their help, then headed off to the schoolyard.

Sal was thumping his baseball into his glove when he suddenly stopped. "I know where I heard that name!" he cried.

"Huh?" I asked. "What're you on about?"

"Armstrong! The name!" he said excitedly. "I remember now! That name was on a lot of gravestones at the Indian cemetery!"

"Oh, yeah, you're right," I said. "That means the Armstrongs Susie stayed with might have been Wyandots!"

"What if Samuel actually knew them?" said Sal.

"I guess we'll never really know," I said, but down deep I wanted to believe he did.

Sofi and I played with Coco and Butterscotch while Sal and Ollie practiced pitching. When they finished, Ollie got in one of the swings, pumped as high as he could, and bailed out.

"Are you really trying to kill yourself?" I asked. Sometimes I don't know what is wrong with him! "Come on, let's go have lunch so we can be ready to go see Granny."

Chapter 16
Clues from the Diary

That afternoon, Mom drove us to Grandma and Grandpa's house to see Granny. She was sitting in a stuffed chair, looking out the window of the extra bedroom. The footlocker was on the floor beside her. Mom gave her a hug and introduced Sal and Sofi. Granny is so tiny, hardly taller than Ollie, and I was afraid to hug her in case I might hurt her.

"Land sakes, Orion," said Granny. "What did you do to your hair?" But she smiled when she said it. "Ollie, you're growing like a weed," she added.

We all sat on the floor beside the locker. Ollie didn't waste any time. He opened the locker and took out the box of medals.

"Granny, tell me about the medals!" he said. "What

are they for? Was my great-grandpa a war hero?" He handed her the box.

"He never felt like a hero," said Granny. "He saved a man's life in Belgium, and later he got shot in the arm, but he just wanted that war to be over so he could come home."

"But didn't he like fighting the enemy? That would be so cool!" said Ollie.

"Oh, really?" said Mom, shaking her head.

"Your great-grandpa thought the war was terrible," said Granny. "It was cold and muddy over there, he didn't understand the language, and he never knew if he'd make it back alive."

Granny picked up the cloth patch with a black panther on it. "This is the emblem of the Black Panthers," she said. "Lincoln was proud to be part of that regiment." (Lincoln Hawthorn was my great-grandpa's name.) She picked up the gold-colored heart with a purple ribbon over it. "And this is the Purple Heart he got for being wounded."

"Sweet!" said Sal. "So he *was* a hero." Ollie wanted to pin the medal on his T-shirt and Granny said it was OK.

I had to roll my eyes. "It doesn't make *you* a hero," I told him.

I was wondering how we were going to talk to Granny about Susie with Mom sitting there. Granny must have read my mind, because she said, "Kathleen, do you know where your dad keeps his old Army things? Ollie might like to see them."

"I can go look," said Mom. She started up the steps to Grandpa and Grandma's bedroom.

"Grandpa Louie was in a war?" asked Ollie. He was practically jumping up and down.

"Not now!" I said. "This is our chance to talk to Granny about...you know..." We crowded a little closer to Granny. She patted Ollie on the head.

"So, Granny," I said, not knowing quite how to start, "did you ever notice anything...strange...about your house? I mean, the one you just moved out of? We've been helping Grandma and Grandpa clean it out."

Granny tilted her head. "What's strange about it?" she asked.

"Well...did you ever hear or see anything that seemed weird?" I said.

"Did anybody else ever live there with you?" asked Sal.

"Why do you think that?" asked Granny.

"Well," I went on, "we went to the attic, and it was all fixed up like an old-fashioned bedroom..."

Granny looked thoughtful for a minute, then said, "I figure you must have seen or heard something, else you wouldn't be asking questions." She looked at each of us. "Can you kids keep a secret?"

We all nodded and moved even closer to her chair.

Granny pointed to the footlocker and said, "Bring me the diary." *OMG*, I thought, she *does* know something, and she's going to tell us! Sal grabbed the diary out of the locker and handed it to Granny.

Granny took a deep breath. "This diary was written by my grandma, Mattie Briggs." She held it up to her heart. "I haven't read it in a long time, but I remember it tells about her daddy, Ezekiel."

"Ezekiel!" I cried, and Granny stopped talking and looked at me funny. "Ooops, sorry," I mumbled. My brain was trying to wrap itself around what I'd just heard. *Mattie Briggs was Granny's grandma?! And her dad's name was Ezekiel? Could this be...?*

"Ezekiel was a slave on a farm in Missouri. His wife and young daughter escaped from their owner, and he was planning to run away and join them, but his master, Mr. Briggs, came to get him the night he was going to leave. Mr. Briggs took Ezekiel and another slave to town with him to do some business.

"Now Ezekiel couldn't very well run away when he was with Mr. Briggs. And when they got back to the farm, word came from the neighbors that Ezekiel's wife and daughter had run away. He knew Mr. Briggs'd be watching him extra-close to make sure he didn't run away too."

Ezekiel worked for Mr. Briggs—now I was sure! The diary was telling about Susie's father!

"Ezekiel didn't dare run away then, because Mr. Briggs might follow him and find his wife and girl, too. Then they'd all be brought back and punished. So Ezekiel just sat tight, hoping for a chance to sneak away. The thing was, his wife was going to have a baby, and he wanted to be with them.

"Anyway, he never got a good chance to escape, and he still didn't know if his wife and daughter made it to the north safe. And then the war broke out. You know, the war between the north and the south."

"We do!" I said. "We learned about it in history at school!"

Granny went on. "Well, by and by, the slaves got freed, and Ezekiel came here to Kansas and joined the Union Army. He still hoped he could find his wife and daughter. Soon as he could, he traveled all around the area, asking if anyone knew about them."

"What was his wife's name?" I asked, holding my breath until she answered.

"It was kind of unusual. If I remember right, her name was Birdie," said Granny. I was so excited I clapped my hands! "Well, by that time Quindaro was starting to die out and folks were moving away. Ezekiel finally did find some people who had known about Birdie, but they had to break the bad news to him: Birdie and her daughter, and a baby girl, had all died before he got there. Ezekiel was heartbroken. He never even got to see the baby girl."

"But wait!" said Sal. "Ezekiel would have been *your* great-grandfather!"

"That's right," said Granny. "Ezekiel stayed around Quindaro, and started working at the sawmill, saving his money, and he finally met a woman and got married again. That woman was my great-grandma, Cassie Briggs."

Yikes! I could hardly take all this in!

"Whoa!" said Ollie. "You know what that means? Ezekiel was *my* great-great-great…how many greats? Grandfather!"

"Mine, too!" I said. I counted up the "greats" and got to four! "He was our great-great-great-great grandpa!"

"Is this all written in the diary?" asked Sal.

Granny nodded. "Ezekiel didn't write it down, of course. He didn't know how to read or write. But his daughter Mattie wrote it all down, right here. That's how we know the family history."

"That's a super story," said Sal, "but why is it a secret?"

"Oh, that's not the secret," said Granny. "The secret's about Ezekiel's daughter…the one who ran away."

Chapter 17

Granny's Secret

"Now, this part's not in the diary," Granny said. "Some of it I've heard through the grapevine, but some was told to me by people who would know. You kids are the first ones I ever told…and probably the last."

"Through the grapevine?" asked Ollie. "Is that what you used to use for telephones?"

"It just means it's like a rumor, or gossip," said Sal. "Let her go on!"

"Back when the town of Quindaro started up, they say, a family by the name of Armstrong took in a woman and a little girl who'd escaped from slavery. The woman had a baby while she was waitin' for her husband to come and meet them. But he never came, and the woman and her children died.

"Now Mrs. Armstrong couldn't even talk about the woman and the children staying in her house, 'cause it was against the law to hide slaves who'd escaped. Then when they died, Mrs. Armstrong just shut up the room they'd lived in, and never used it again. Not long after, Quindaro started to die out, and everybody moved on to higher ground, away from the river. All the old houses got torn down, or just fell down. The Armstrongs built a new house, but they took the things from the slave woman's room with them, and set them up in the attic."

"But why?" asked Ollie. "They were all dead!"

"Well," said Granny, "they say Mrs. Armstrong had a funny feeling about the room…like somebody was still there. She thought she heard a young girl singing to a baby in there, rocking it to sleep, but when she'd open the door, there was nobody there. Mrs. Armstrong didn't go inside the room, 'cause it kind of spooked her, but she felt so bad about them dying before the husband could find them, it just seemed right to leave the room like it was, in memory of them."

"She never saw anybody, ever?" asked Sal.

"Not ever. But the house stayed in the Armstrong family for years, and they always kept that attic room fixed just like it was when the woman and her children were there. Guess they figured if there was a spirit or somethin' up there, it needed a place to stay."

"You're telling us the house was haunted!" said Sal.

"I suppose I am," said Granny. She looked at each of us. "So you see why I never talked about this before, and why I asked you keep it a secret?"

We all looked at each other, wide-eyed. "So how did you come to find out about all this?" I finally asked.

"Well," said Granny, "I grew up near old Quindaro, and I'd heard the talk about the old Armstrong house for years. And I knew from readin' my grandma's diary that Ezekiel had come to find his wife and daughter, but got here too late. I didn't know for sure if they were the ones staying with the Armstrongs, but I wanted to find out. Then after Lincoln died and my kids were grown, I had a chance to buy the house.

"It was old Mrs. Armstrong's great grand-daughter who'd lived there, and I asked her about the rumors. I told her there might be a connection with my own great-grandpa. She'd never heard about a man named Ezekiel, but she knew the woman who'd stayed there was named Birdie, and there was a daughter and a baby. She'd heard about them from her own mother and grandmother. She showed me the room in the attic and said she hoped I'd keep it the same, and I said I would.

"Well, when I heard the woman's name was Birdie, I was sure she was Ezekiel's wife. And that girl, the one they heard singing to the baby, was Ezekiel's daughter. She would've been the half-sister of my grandma Mattie, who wrote the diary. That girl was my great-auntie."

My jaw dropped. She was talking about Susie! Susie was my granny's great-aunt!

"Did *you* ever see or hear anybody?" I asked.

"Did you hear a girl singing?" asked Ollie.

"I never did," said Granny, "and I didn't want to disturb whoever might be there. I just kept the stairway door closed and only went up to air out the attic once in a while."

"Did you ever talk to Mrs. Armstrong's great-granddaughter again about Birdie?" asked Sal.

Granny shook her head. "She passed away soon after, I heard. She was in her 90s."

"So…Birdie and her kids never knew that Ezekiel did come to Kansas to find them," said Sal.

"Well, I think that's what's behind the rumors," said Granny. "There's an old saying from slave times, you know—it says if you don't die satisfied, you have to come back. Now I never believed the stories of spirits and haints and all—"

"What are haints?" asked Ollie.

"Oh, you know, ghosts and such," said Granny. "But the older I get, the more I think that's right…that young girl just couldn't die satisfied 'cause she never knew about Ezekiel."

"And so she came back!" said Ollie.

"But if you thought there was somebody in the attic,

didn't you want to tell them that Ezekiel came to find them?" I asked.

"Maybe I should have," said Granny. "I'd think about just going up there and telling the story, as I knew it, but then I'd feel kind of silly, talking in an empty room. But I could have let them know, even if it didn't do any good. It wouldn't have hurt me none. Now I suppose they'll be left wondering and waiting, for all eternity." She looked a little sad.

"I wish there was a way we could tell her!" cried Ollie. I gave him a look to shut him up. We needed to talk this over before we said any more to Granny.

"You didn't even tell Grandpa about this?" I asked.

"Lord, no, child! He and his sisters were all bent on getting their education, and they never went along with those old stories. Louis would think I was losing my mind," said Granny sadly. "And maybe I am…but I feel better now that I told somebody about it."

"What's going to happen when you sell the house?" asked Sal. "What'll happen if it gets torn down?"

"Grandpa says he's gonna take the stuff out of the attic and get rid of it!" I said.

Right then Mom came back downstairs, carrying Grandpa's old Army coat and some photos. Sal put the diary back into the footlocker as Mom came into the room.

"Granny, you look worn out!" said my mom when she saw Granny's face. "Are you feeling OK? I hope these kids haven't pestered you too much!"

"They've been good as gold," said Granny. She gave a weak smile, but she *did* look pretty tired. Mom showed us the things she'd found from when Grandpa was in the Army.

"Did he get shot?" asked Ollie.

"No," said Mom. "That's a good thing, you know."

"I guess so," said Ollie, but he looked disappointed.

We visited for a few more minutes, then Mom went to put away Grandpa's Army things. After she left the room, Granny said, "Remember, what I told you is a secret. Are you sure you can keep it?"

"Absolutely!" I said, and everyone agreed. Right before we left, I remembered something.

"Granny," I said, "whose harmonica is that in the locker?"

"Oh, that was Ezekiel's," she said. "My great-grand-daddy was said to be quite the musician."

Chapter 18

Orion Needs a Break

Talk about bad timing! Now that Granny had dropped the bombshell about Susie's dad, we'd probably never see her again! We needed a way to get back to Granny's house, but we were running out of time. The next day was Friday, the last weekday of spring break. Sal and Sofi were spending the day with their mom. Taylor and Mady would be back from their trips, and we were going to sleep over at Mady's that night. Just a few days ago, I'd been so excited to see my friends and show off my hair, but now all I could think about was how to see Susie again.

Friday morning I had to stay busy to keep from going crazy. It was sunny and warm, so I rode my bike to the schoolyard. I needed some time alone to try out a new idea. A couple of weeks before break, when our class was running outside in gym class, Miss Henderson had told me I should think about running track in middle school. She said I have a good stride and strong turnover. How cool is that? I mean, Sal's good at baseball, and Sofi's good at gymnastics, and Ollie *thinks* he's good at Ninja Warrior stuff, but me? I'm not into any of that, so maybe running could be *my* thing.

I ran all the way around the school yard, stopped to catch my breath, and did it again. My legs were tired, but honest, I felt really great! I was on my third lap around when Ollie, Sal and Sofi arrived. Ollie and Sal had their baseball gloves. I finished my lap and went to the swings with Sofi. When the boys finished throwing, they came and sat with us.

"You gonna be a track star?" asked Sal. "You're pretty fast." His baseball made a *thunk! thunk*! sound as he threw it into his glove.

"Maybe," I said. "I might start training."

"So," he said, "you know we *have* to find a way to tell Susie what your Granny told us!"

"But when?" I said. "I've got a sleepover with Mady and Taylor tonight, then it's the weekend, and then we'll have to go back to school!"

"Don't you want her to be able to go back to her grave?" he asked.

"I do! I just can't think of a good reason to go back to the house!"

"Could we say we left something there?" asked Ollie.

"Like what?" I said. "If we left something, Grandpa would just bring it to us. And we can't tell him why we really want to go back!"

"Well, we have to think of something!" said Sal. "Otherwise—"

"I wonder what they're gonna do with the stuff in the attic?" said Ollie. "I wish I could have the mirror!"

"But Susie needs it," I said.

"Well, if we leave it there, Grandpa said it'd just get thrown away," he said.

"That's right," said Sal. "So we have to somehow talk to Susie again before the mirror ends up in some dumpster."

"I know, but I'm out of ideas!" I cried.

AFTER LUNCH I went up to my room to rest a bit. My head was spinning from trying to come up with a way to see Susie again. I packed my stuff for the sleepover at Mady's and flopped down on my bed to think. Funny, I'd thought the things Granny told us would answer all my questions, but now I had even more. I made a list in my head:

1.   If we tell Susie about Ezekiel, can she die satisfied?

2. Will she go back to her grave? Where *is* her grave, anyway?
3. What *will* happen to Susie if her things get sold or thrown away?
4. Should we tell Granny about Susie?
5. What is that tap-tap-tapping I hear, and why won't it stop?

"Orion? Orion! Mady's here! Are you all ready?" It was my mom, knocking on my bedroom door. I must have fallen asleep!

"Coming!" I yelled, and grabbed my backpack. I ran downstairs, where Mady and her mother were waiting in the front hall. Mady had a cool suntan from her week in Florida.

"My, look at your hair!" said Mrs. Peterson.

"WHOAAA!" said Mady. "I didn't know you were gonna do streaks! Come on, we've gotta pick up Taylor, and then we're going for pizza!"

It felt great to hang out, laugh, eat and talk to my friends after worrying about Susie all week. Mady told us all about Florida, and when we got back to her house, she gave Taylor and me each a seashell from Amelia Island. We saw photos of Mady and her older sister on the beach, in the water, and under palm trees. Taylor talked about visiting her cousins in Tulsa. Her aunt spoke Spanish to her the whole time she was there, and she's getting really good at it. I can't lie, even though

I'd met Susie, I was a little jealous that I'd been stuck at home the whole week.

"What about you?" Taylor asked. "Did you do anything fun this week?"

"Well…," I started. I couldn't tell them I met a ghost, so I said, "I helped my grandparents clean out my great-grandma's house so they can sell it. And we found a box of medals my great-grandpa got in the war, and… and I learned my four-times great grandpa was an actual slave!"

Taylor's eyes got round. "Are you serious?" she asked. "He was a slave? That is so awesome!"

"Well, actually, it kind of sucked," I said. "Being a slave, I mean. I learned a whole lot about slavery, so I can do my report for Ms. Patel!"

"Ugh!" said Mady. "I don't even want to think about the history report! Now I'll have to figure out something to write about!"

"We've only got two more days of break!" said Taylor. "Let's just have fun and not talk about school!"

Chapter 19
Too Late to Help Susie?

The sleepover helped take my mind off Susie for a while, but coming home was a real downer. I had to wash the streaks out of my hair, and practice flute, which I should have been doing all week, and be ready for school on Monday. Instead, I sat on my bed and thought about Susie. What if we couldn't find a way to tell her what was in the diary about Ezekiel—could she *ever* die satisfied and go back to her grave?

I looked at my drawing of Susie. Just to keep busy, I turned to another page in my sketch pad and started drawing, trying to get her different expressions from memory. I needed one with her smiling. I got the outline of her face down, and started putting in the features, her pretty eyes, her long lashes, her dimples…*OMG! Susie has dimples, and she's Granny's great-aunt!* I took my sketch pad and ran to Ollie's room.

"Look!" I cried. "You noticed Susie has dimples, right? Just like us?"

"Yeah, so?" he said.

"Well, Granny told us Susie's her great-aunt! She's our great-great-whatever aunt, too! The dimples must be a family trait! You know? Like Dad says the way our hair grows in a point on our foreheads is an O'Brien family trait!" (It's called a widow's peak. Don't ask me why.)

"Yeah, I guess so," he said. "But now that we know Susie's our aunt, we've *gotta* tell her about Ezekiel! We can't just let her wonder about him forever, can we?"

"But what can we do?" I asked. It seemed pretty hopeless.

Sunday, the last day of break, I ran a couple of laps at the playground, played with Butterscotch in the back yard, and worked on my pictures of Susie. I should have checked over my homework, but I didn't feel like it. I kept trying to think of some way we could go to Granny's house once more, but I came up empty. I was in a pretty bad mood when Mom told me to go to the back yard and get Ollie for dinner. He was sitting on the platform in the tree.

"Get down here now!" I said. "Don't you know what time it is?"

"Why are you being such a grouch?" asked Ollie as he swung down from the tree on the rope. "Sal never talks to Sofi like that."

"Well, Sofi's not a pain in the butt like you are," I said.

"I'm telling Mom," he started, but I didn't care.

"So go ahead and tell her," I said. We both went in for dinner without another word.

"All ready for school tomorrow?" asked Dad. "You had a pretty good break after all, didn't you?"

I shrugged. "I guess so."

"I got lots of practice on my Ninja Warrior moves and my pitching," said Ollie. "I hope it doesn't rain again for a while so I can get really good!"

"Grandpa called this morning and said you kids were a big help at Granny's house," said Mom.

"Yeah, we did a lot," said Ollie.

"*We?*" I said. "*You* mostly played with Sofi and Co..."

"But is there something you haven't told us about a cat?" asked Mom. "Didn't I see Sofi with a kitten in the back yard?"

"I didn't do anything!" said Ollie.

"Uh, well," I said, looking at Mom, "there was a stray kitten, and Sofi really wanted to keep her, and she knew we weren't going back to the house, so she kind of... just...brought her home."

"Why didn't you tell Grandma you were taking her?" asked Dad.

"Honest, we didn't even know until we were on our way home!" I said.

"Is Grandpa mad?" asked Ollie.

"No, but he wondered why the kitten stopped showing up, and then Grandma noticed the cat food was gone."

Uh-oh, busted...I should have thought of that! "Could we go back to the house just one more time, maybe tomorrow after school?" I was desperate. "I'll tell Grandpa I'm sorry about the kitten, and help him finish packing up."

"You do need to explain about the kitten," said Mom, "but they're all finished at the house. All that's left is for the junk truck to come and haul away what's left."

I looked up. "You mean...they're taking everything out of the house? Now?"

"Tomorrow," she answered.

I looked at Ollie. At first he just stared back, but then he gasped. "Even the attic?" he asked.

"Grandpa said there was nothing up there worth saving," said Mom. "Anyway, they have to get everything out because the house goes on the market this week."

Could things get any worse? I felt like I might puke up my dinner. I excused myself and said I had to get ready for school. Ollie came up the steps behind me and I yanked him into my room.

"What're we gonna do?" he asked. "What if they throw the mirror away?"

"And what about the humpback chest with the doll in it?" I wailed. "How can Susie wait for her dad if they take her things away?" Poor Susie...her whole world would be torn apart, and she couldn't die satisfied, and we'd never be able to find out what happened to her. I had no idea how to get out of this. I finally shoved Ollie out of my room and got ready for bed. No way was I going to let my little brother see me cry.

"Time to get up, Orion!" called Mom. "First day back at school, don't be late!"

I opened my eyes and felt excited to be going back to see all my friends...then I remembered the night before, and what Mom had told me about Susie's things at Granny's house. I got dressed, and on the way down the stairs, I stopped Ollie and said, "Eat your breakfast fast, so we can go over and talk to Sal before school."

"You both seem pretty excited about going back," said Mom as we scarfed down our cereal.

"I'm gonna go over and walk with Sal," said Ollie as he grabbed his backpack. "Bye, Mom!"

We ran across the street and stood on the Martellis' porch. Sofi saw us through the window and came out a moment later. Sal followed close behind.

"We've got a big problem," I said. "Grandpa told Mom they've got Granny's house all emptied out now, and they're ready to haul everything off."

"Mom said they're taking everything from the attic," said Ollie.

"But what about Susie?" asked Sofi. "What if they take her doll?"

Sal thought for a minute. "We have to just call your grandpa and ask him to keep the mirror and the chest," he said. "Can we go do it now?"

"OK, come on, I'll tell Mom I forgot something!" I yelled, as I started back across the street. The others all ran after me. I crashed through the front door just as Mom was coming out of the kitchen.

"What are you doing, Orion?" she asked. "You're going to be late!"

"I forgot my—" I shouted, and ran toward the stairs.

"You have four minutes until the bell rings," said Mom. "What did you forget?"

I stopped halfway up the stairs. I should have known it was too late. No way would we have enough time to make a phone call and explain to Grandpa what we needed. "Uh, I've got everything!" I said as we all dashed back out the door.

We ran all the way to school. When we stopped by the front step, out of breath, I asked, "But what if Susie's stuff goes to the dumpster?"

"Yeah, what if the mirror gets broken?" asked Ollie. "Does that mean it'll hurt Susie?"

"We'll just have to do it after school," said Sal. "Just hope for the best."

I TRIED TO ENJOY SEEING all my classmates and hearing what everyone did over break, but it was the longest day of my life! I zoned out more than once after lunch during geography. I couldn't wait to get home and call Grandpa. As soon as the last bell rang, I started for home without even waiting for Ollie. As I turned up our block, he, Sal and Sofi came running up behind me.

"You couldn't even wait for us?" said Ollie.

"It's too important—come on!"

We hurried through the front door. "Hi, Mom!" I yelled on my way up the stairs. "We'll be down in a minute!

"Grandpa's landline's on speed dial," I said as I punched in the number "1" on the upstairs phone. "I hope he's home!" Everyone waited nervously as the phone rang. And rang. And rang.

Chapter 20
Granny and Grandpa to the Rescue

Sofi and Ollie were both holding their breath, and Sal was looking at me hopefully, but I was about to give up. I shook my head and started to hang up the phone when, FINALLY, someone picked up.

"Hello?" said a shaky-sounding voice. Did I get the wrong number? Wait, I speed-dialed it!

"Granny?" I said. "It's Orion. Is Grandpa there?"

The others all crowded in close, but Granny's voice was so quiet they couldn't hear.

"Turn on the speaker!" said Sal. Why didn't I think of that? We turned the volume up as high as it would go.

"Hi, Granny," I said. "I'm here with Ollie and our friends Sal and Sofi, the ones who came to see you? We need to talk to Grandpa."

"He's not here now," said Granny. "I'll ask him to call you as soon as he gets home."

"But we need to tell him something, right now!" said Ollie.

"It's really important!" I said. "Remember when we talked about the attic room in your house? And you told us the rumors about the girl singing to a baby?"

Granny started to say something, but Ollie broke in. "We need the mirror!" he cried.

"Please?" I said. "We've gotta tell him to save the mirror and the humpback chest. Is there any way you can get hold of him and tell him?"

"Well, he's over at the house right now, meeting the man with the junk truck," said Granny. "He said everything left would be hauled away. I'll see what I can do. Are you going to tell me why that mirror's so important?"

"It's a matter of life or death!" said Ollie.

"I promise we'll tell you everything!" I said. "Just tell Grandpa we need it as soon as possible!"

Granny said she would do her best, and hung up.

"Life or death?" I said to Ollie.

"Well, sort of," he answered back. "It might mean everything for Susie."

"He's right," said Sal. "All we can do now is wait."

AFTER DINNER I WENT UP to my room and tried to concentrate on the things coming up for the week—soccer, new music for band, math competitions—but all I could do was listen for the phone. I was brushing my teeth when I heard it ring.

"Orion! Grandpa's on the phone—he wants to talk to you," called Mom.

I gulped a drink of water and swallowed my toothpaste. "I'll get it up here!" I ran to the phone in Mom's room as fast as I could, but Ollie had already picked it up. I yanked it out of his hand.

"Hello, Grandpa?" I turned on the speaker so Ollie could hear.

"Granny said you want some things out of her house," he said. "The mirror in the attic, and that little chest?"

"Did they get thrown away?" asked Ollie.

"Well, you got lucky, because the man had just loaded the stuff from the attic on his truck when Granny called my cell phone," he said. "I got the mirror and chest off the truck, and they're in my garage now."

"Oh, thank you, Grandpa!" I cried. "You don't know how happy you've made me!"

"Well, it's no problem, I just can't figure out why you want that old stuff," he said.

"I want the mirror in my room," said Ollie. "It's fun! We can look in it and act silly and crazy and show all our friends!"

"And there's some stuff in the chest that we thought

Granny'd like to see," I said. "Can you bring them over?"

"I can do it later this week," said Grandpa. He paused. "Is there something else you wanted to tell me?"

"What? Oh," I said, "about the kitten...Sofi loved her so much, she hid her inside her jacket and brought her home. We didn't even know it until we got here!"

"Did anybody call you about a lost kitten?" asked Ollie.

"No, nobody called. I know Sofi loves her, but I wish she'd just asked before taking her."

"I know," I said. "I'm real sorry...but thank you, Grandpa. I love you!"

BOY, WAS IT HARD, waiting for Grandpa to bring Susie's things! Being back in school helped keep my mind off Susie, and afternoons I stayed busy running laps at the playground and playing with Butterscotch. Ollie was back into Ninja Warrior mode and started begging Dad to build him a salmon ladder, like on American Ninja Warrior, for his birthday.

Friday afternoon, right before dinner, Grandpa Louie came and brought the mirror. Mom made us clean it off in the garage, then Grandpa helped us take it upstairs to Ollie's room. "What about the chest?" I asked.

"I thought you said Granny should see it," he said. "I left it at home, but you can get it next time you're over there."

"Uh, OK," I said. I tried not to look disappointed. At least it didn't go to the dumpster!

After dinner, Mom went up to Ollie's room to look at the mirror.

"This is what you wanted so bad?" she asked. "I can see why Grandpa was going to throw it out."

"But it's so fun!" said Ollie as he clowned in front of the mirror.

"Well, just be careful with it," said Mom. "We don't need an old *broken* mirror."

Chapter 21
A Surprise Visit

Something was shaking my shoulder.

"Orion! Orion, wake up!" It was Ollie, whispering to me.

"What? Go away!" I turned over and pulled the sheet over my head.

He shook harder. "Wake up! I gotta tell you something!"

I sat up in bed. "What are you doing?! It's the middle of the night! I'm gonna kill—!"

"SHHHH!" he whispered. "Don't wake Mom and Dad up! Come over to my room! I think Susie's there!"

That woke me up fast. I jumped out of bed and went quietly over to his room. He had his lamp on, and the wall clock said 11:49. Ollie grabbed my arm and pulled me down in front of the mirror.

"Listen!" he whispered.

"I don't hear anything!" I whispered, and was about to go back to my room, but then I heard it—somebody singing, very quietly.

Hush-a-bye, don't you cry...

"Susie!" I whispered. "Are you here? Come and talk to us!"

Go to sleepy, little baby...

"Susie!" I whispered. "I know you're there! Can you come to see us?"

Nothing happened. I looked at Ollie. He was staring at the mirror and then he tugged my arm and pointed. In the dim lamp light, all I could see were Susie's big, dark eyes.

"There she is!" he cried. I looked hard and could just make out her shape in the mirror. It wasn't like a real reflection, more like looking through fog or something.

"SSHHHHH!" I whispered. "Susie? Can't you come?" We sat waiting, but Susie never got any clearer.

"What should we do?" asked Ollie.

I thought for a minute. "Susie," I said, "I think you're trying to tell us that you can't come out all the way. Is there anything we can do to help?"

She looked so hazy in the mirror, it was hard to see what she was doing, but she folded her arms in front of her and swayed them back and forth.

"She's rocking a baby?" said Ollie. "She wants to rock…the doll! She wants us to get the doll!"

"Is that what you want, Susie?" I asked. She didn't answer, so I said, "OK, Susie, we'll do our best. I'll ask my grandpa to bring the doll so you can see it."

As we watched, Susie disappeared into the mirror.

"You know what this means?" I said to Ollie as soon as Susie was gone.

"She can talk to us here and we can tell her Granny's secret!" he said. "We've gotta get the doll!"

I HAD TO DRAG OUT OF BED Saturday morning to be ready for my soccer game. I'd stayed awake for hours after seeing Susie in the mirror, trying to figure out what we should do. I'd decided on two things: we had to get the doll out of the humpback chest ASAP, and we had to tell Granny about Susie.

I found Mom in the kitchen.

"You know, Grandma was right about Granny," I said. "She knows a lot about the family. Could we talk to her again soon? I really want to know about her great-grandpa who was a slave."

Mom said, "I don't see why not. Not everybody has a great-grandma they can talk to."

I called Sal on the upstairs phone. "Can you come

over right away? We've got something really important to tell you, but I can't talk about it on the phone!"

I met them at the front door and we went to the back yard.

"You won't believe what happened last night!" I said. "Remember how Ollie wanted the mirror from Granny's house? Well, Grandpa brought it over last night, and…"

"And I heard Susie singing in my room!" Ollie finished.

"No way!" said Sal.

"Way!" yelled Ollie.

"So that means she got out of your granny's house? But where is she...in Ollie's room?"

"Well, the mirror's in his room," I said. "So maybe wherever the mirror is, that's where she is...or at least, where we can see her."

Sal was quiet for a minute, then said, "O-o-h, I get it. The mirror's not for Susie, it's for us...it's like her gateway to the outside!"

"And nobody ever looked in it before us!" said Ollie.

"And now it's in Ollie's room, so she came to see us!" I said. I pointed up to Ollie's window.

"Yeah, I was in bed, and I heard someone singing that 'Hush-a-bye' song, and I thought for sure I was dreaming, but it kept up, and I woke up and it was for real," said Ollie. "So I turned on my lamp and looked in the mirror, but I couldn't see anybody."

"So he came and got me, and we both looked, and we finally saw Susie…that is, her eyes, the rest of her was hardly there, just sort of…foggy," I finished.

"Did she talk to you?" asked Sal.

"No!" I said. "I mean, I don't think she could."

"She went like this," said Ollie, and showed Sal and Sofi how Susie had swayed her arms like she was rocking a baby. "I think it means she wants the doll!" he said.

"The doll will help her talk to us," said Sofi.

We all looked at her. As usual, when Sofi says something, it's important.

"So if the mirror's the gateway, the doll brings her through?" said Sal.

"Oh, I get it!" I said. "The doll's really for *us*—it makes it so she can talk to us."

"Yeah," said Sal, "at your Granny's, the mirror and all her stuff were together in one room, but now—"

"The chest is at my grandpa's house," I said. "We have to go get it."

"It'll give us a chance to tell Susie what your granny said! And we're gonna tell your granny about Susie, right?" said Sal.

"Well, we promised to tell her why we needed the mirror, so we don't have a choice!" I said. "And Granny told us *her* secret…now it's time to tell her ours!"

Chapter 22
Susie Gets Outed

Mom was taking us to see Granny Sunday afternoon. She said Granny had enjoyed our last visit, but warned us that she was getting weaker. We promised we wouldn't wear her out.

"Are you sure Sal and Sofi want to go?" asked Mom.

"Absolutely!" I said. "Sal and I are both using stuff from her diary for our reports." I know, this was technically not true, but I couldn't tell Mom where Sal *really* got his information, could I?

"Well, this'll work fine, because Grandpa wants me to look at some papers they need for selling the house," she said. "We can do that while you're with Granny."

Granny seemed even smaller than the last time we saw her, which was only last week! We sat down in front of her while Mom went to the kitchen with Grandma and Grandpa.

"Granny," I said, "you told us you grew up near Quindaro, right?"

"That's right," she said.

"Did you know it was a station on the underground railroad?" asked Ollie.

"That's what I always heard," she said. "It was a jumping-off place for runaway slaves to stop on their way north. They wanted to get as far away from the south as they could, some even went to Canada."

"So do you know where the "station" was?" asked Ollie.

"Not for sure," said Granny. "Could've been the old Wyandot Hotel, or maybe the old brewery. They say the brewery had a chute that went down to the river, where they hauled up ice in the winter. Supposed to be how they snuck in runaway slaves."

"Awesome!" said Ollie.

"Do you think Ezekiel's wife and daughter came on the underground railroad?" I asked.

"Well," said Granny, "I've always believed that. I don't know how else they could've got here—a woman and girl travelin' alone, it would have been real dangerous. Lots of slaves tried to run away, but only a few made it—mostly the ones who came from the Border States, like Missouri, close by."

"Did the Indians help them?" asked Ollie.

"Well, some did," said Granny. "The woman I bought the house from said her grandma, who took in Birdie and her girl, was Indian. The land used to belong to some Indian tribes, you know."

"Granny," I said, keeping my voice low, "remember when you asked us if we could keep a secret? Well, we've got a secret, too...and you're the only person we can tell!"

"It's about why we needed the mirror from the attic!" said Ollie. "And now we need something out of the chest, the one Grandpa got off the junk truck for us."

"Oh?" she said. "It's over by the window. I haven't looked in it."

Sal picked up the chest and set it near Granny's feet.

"Well," I began, "it's about the rumor that there was somebody in the attic of your house."

"About the girl singing and rocking a baby to sleep?" said Ollie.

"Right," I said. "And you were pretty sure it had to be your great-grandpa's daughter, who died before he could find her."

"You were right!" cried Ollie.

"Keep your voice down!" I said to him. I didn't want Mom or Grandpa coming in to see what was going on!

"Well, there *was* a girl in the attic. We saw her, and we know who she is!"

Granny was very still for a minute. "What exactly did you see?" she asked.

"A slave girl named Susanna…Susie…who escaped from her owner and came to Quindaro on the underground railroad with her mother. They were gonna wait until her dad could come and meet them, and then go to Canada," I said.

"Her mom's name was Birdie and her dad was Ezekiel," said Sal.

"Her mom had a baby after they got here," said Sofi.

"And they kept waiting, but he never came," said Sal, "then they all died of the measles, so they never knew if he got away from his owner and tried to find them."

"Oh, my word," said Granny. "This…Susanna…you really *saw* her?"

"Well…I think…I think it's her ghost," I said. "Like, her spirit."

"In the attic at your house!" said Ollie. "Not for real, but we could see her in the mirror, so that's why we wanted to keep it!"

"She told us she came out of her grave to wait for her daddy, and sometimes she pretends to rock her baby sister to sleep, and sings to her," I added.

"She rocks her sister's doll," said Sofi.

"So that's what it was," said Granny. "I never thought…and how did you get her to talk to you?"

"She saw us when we went to the attic to play," I said. "She thought Ollie and I were slaves, and we might know something about her dad."

"Anyway, Grandpa brought me the mirror," said Ollie, "and we could hear Susie singing, but we couldn't really see her, except for her eyes, so maybe if we have her doll, we can see her and talk to her."

"The doll's in Susie's sewing chest," I said.

Sal opened the top of the chest. Inside we saw the doll, the sampler Susie made, and her other sewing things. Sofi took the doll out and held it up to Granny. I laid the sampler on her lap.

"And look at this—Susie stitched this sampler for her mom and dad," I said. "She knew how to make clothes and sew all kinds of things."

"What else did she tell you?" asked Granny.

"Lots of things!" said Ollie. "All about what it was like to be a slave!"

"And how she and her mom ran away because her brothers had been sold, and her mom was afraid she'd get sold, too," said Sal. "One of them was only seven years old."

"And she came to Quindaro on the underground railroad," I said. "She stayed with a lady named Mrs. Armstrong."

"The same family you bought the house from," said Sal.

"And her dad played the harmonica!" said Sofi.

Granny smoothed the sampler with her fingers. "Such beautiful needlework," she said. "Much as I don't want to believe it, I don't know how you could've known all this…unless she told you." She almost seemed to be talking to herself. "And the names…the harmonica…it all fits together."

"So can we take the doll?" I asked. "To help Susie?" I held my breath, waiting for Granny to answer.

"Susie was my great-auntie," she whispered, "the one I read about in the diary. And now she's waiting to find out what happened to her daddy! Did you tell her?"

"No!" I said. "We never went back to your house after you told us your secret. But now she's trying to talk to us again, and that's why we need the doll. The mirror's not enough."

"And once we tell her about Ezekiel, maybe she can go back to her grave," said Sal.

"Back to her grave," said Granny. "She can die satisfied, like the slaves used to say." She thought for a minute, then seemed to make up her mind. "Take the chest with you," she said. "Those are her things. She's been waiting so long, it's time for her to be at peace. And Orion?" Granny gripped my hand. "Give her my love."

We all jumped when Mom came back into the room

with Grandma and Grandpa. "What's all this?" she asked when she saw the humpback chest.

"Just some things I don't need anymore," said Granny. "I told Orion and Ollie they can take the chest home with them."

"Thank you, Granny!" I said. As I looked at her, I realized I'd never thought of her as *really* part of my family, like Mom and Dad and my grandparents. I'd never known how important she was to me. As I said goodbye, I gave her a huge hug.

Chapter 23
Answers for Susie

"It's hard to believe granny's great-grandpa was a slave!" I said as Mom drove us home.

"You wouldn't believe some of the stuff that happened to them!" said Sal.

"Oh, I probably would," said Mom. "It was hard for me to think about those things when I was growing up, and I wanted to believe it was ancient history. But watching you kids talk to Granny, I've realized we have to keep those stories alive and never let them be forgotten."

"Yeah," I said, "knowing about her great-grandpa makes it a lot more real than just reading about it in our history books."

"I'm proud of all of you for talking to Granny about it, and taking an interest in the family," said Mom. "Who knew you'd learn so much over spring break?"

As soon as we got home, we took the humpback chest up to my room. Butterscotch came with us.

"Should we try it?" I asked Sal. "What about Mom and Dad?"

"We'll just have to take a chance, like we did with Samuel those times when my mom and dad were home," said Sal. "We can't keep Susie waiting!"

"OK, let's go for it, and if anyone comes upstairs, we'll tell them we're practicing giving our reports," I said.

Sal took a piece of paper and printed a sign that said, in big red letters, "DO NOT DISTURB". He taped it to Ollie's door.

"It's now or never," he said as we sat down on the floor in front of the mirror.

I propped the doll in front of us. "Susie?" I said. "Can you talk to us?"

I was afraid it wasn't going to work, but then the air got colder and we saw Susie in the mirror, just like back at Granny's house. The doll must have done the trick! Sofi clapped her hands. Butterscotch started to growl. Susie looked afraid.

"Quiet, Butterscotch," said Ollie. "Susie's a friend." He hugged and petted Butterscotch until she calmed down. She whimpered a couple of times, then put her nose down on the floor between her paws.

"Sorry, Susie," I said. "Butterscotch won't hurt you, but she has to get to know you."

144

"She give me a fright," Susie said. "Made me think of the patrollers bringin' out the dogs to hunt down runaways."

"I can't believe you're here!" said Sal. "I thought you lived…I mean, stayed…in Granny's house, but you can come out wherever the mirror is, can't you?"

"Where are we?" she asked, looking around the room. "This ain't Miz Bets's house."

"No, it's our house," said Ollie. "We brought the mirror over here so it wouldn't get thrown away!"

"And then we brought your doll, because we thought it'd help you talk to us," said Sal. "It worked, didn't it?"

"Anyway, Susie, we've got something real important to tell you." I looked nervously at Sal, trying to think how to do this. I should have known Ollie would just blurt it out.

"We talked to our Granny!" he said. "Miss Bets? Remember, you told us she kept your secret? Well, she told us something about your daddy."

Susie got very still. "Miz Bets knowed about my daddy?"

"He came to find you!" shouted Ollie.

"Quiet!" I said. "Right. When the slaves were freed, he came to Kansas to join the Army. Then after the war he went around trying to find you and your mom. He finally found out you all died before he got there."

Looking at her face, I couldn't tell what Susie was thinking. Finally, she asked, "How she know this?"

I wasn't sure how to tell her the next part. I looked at Sal. "It's all written down in a diary. He couldn't follow you right away because Mr. Briggs took him to town with him. The thing is, after he came...and found out you were all dead...he got married again. He had another daughter, and she wrote all about what happened to him," said Sal.

"My Granny still has the diary," I said.

"And Ezekiel was my great-great-great-great grandpa!" said Ollie.

"I hope it doesn't make you sad," I said, "but I thought you'd want to know. He did try to find you."

Susie stood there looking like a deer in the headlights. Then she said, "What y'all mean, he was your great-great...grandpa?"

"Well, Susie," I said, "that's why my great-grandma, Miss Bets, has the diary, because...because Ezekiel was *her* great-grandpa." This part was hard! "After you... died...he had another daughter named Mattie Briggs, and she was my granny's grandma. So, we counted back, and that means he was our great-great-great-great grandpa."

She didn't say anything for a minute, and I saw her wipe her eyes on her sleeve.

"Susie, are you OK?" asked Sal.

"Don't cry!" said Sofi.

Susie sniffled, then lifted her head. "It's just hard to believe, after all this time...don't quite know what to say," she said.

"Please don't be sad! It's good news!" I said. "He got away from Mr. Briggs, and he came to Kansas, and he had a daughter. And *her* granddaughter's my great-grandma! So that makes you Granny's great-aunt!"

"It means you're part of our family!" said Ollie.

Susie's eyes got even bigger and rounder. "Did y'all tell her about me? That I been talkin' to y'all?"

"We had to," said Ollie. "Granny's 94 and she might die soon."

"We did," I said. "My Granny told us a secret about the attic room, how people thought they heard someone singing to a baby, so they kept it the same ever since you and your mom and Rebecca were there. She had a hunch it was you...Ezekiel's daughter...in the room, but she wasn't sure. So we told her about you, because...well, it's true, she won't live forever. She told us to give you her love."

Susie wiped another tear from her face. "Been so long since I had somebody to love me," she said. "If y'all don't mind, I'd like to be by myself for awhile now."

"Sure," said Sal. He looked disappointed, but we all quickly got up and went downstairs.

"Is she mad? Or sad, or what?" asked Ollie.

"I was hoping she'd be happy to know that Ezekiel got away from Mr. Briggs," said Sal.

"I don't know," I said. "Maybe all three."

Chapter 24

Does the Mirror Still Work?

We understood Susie needed some time to think about what we'd told her, and to decide what she was going to do.

"I guess it was a real shock, after all this time," said Sal.

"Will she go back to her grave now?" asked Sofi.

"What if she already did? She might never come out again!" said Ollie.

"That's the problem," I said. "I really wanted her to tell us about running away on the underground railroad, for my report."

"You just want help with that report!" cried Ollie. "Don't you want her to die satisfied?"

I gave him a mean look. I *did* feel a bit guilty about

wishing Susie back just to help me write my report. "Of course, I do!" I said.

"We'd all like to hear about how she escaped," said Sal. "But we have to think about what's best for her. Remember? Like Samuel told us."

"I know, but I just want to tell her how much she means to me and how awesome she is and…."

"And we didn't get to tell her goodbye," said Sofi.

"Could we try just one more time?" I asked. "I mean, you'd like to see her again, too, right? And if she's gone back to her grave, well…I'll be happy for her." I'm not sure I meant it, but still.

We agreed we would try to talk to Susie one more time. I wasn't sure how we were going to pull it off. The reports were due in another week. Sal was almost finished with his, but I hadn't even started mine.

We had to wait until Friday night for our chance. The Martellis came over for barbecue, so after dinner we went up to Ollie's room while our parents talked. I brought the humpback chest from my room. It was almost dark, so we turned on Ollie's lamp and sat down in front of the mirror. We put the sampler and the doll on the floor in front of us. Butterscotch sniffed at them.

"Susie?" I called. "Can you come and talk to us?" We waited.

"What if she doesn't come?" asked Ollie.

Sal shrugged. "All we can do is try," he said.

But then, as we watched, the air around us got cold and Susie appeared in the mirror. Right away I saw there was something different about her. She looked…happier.

"Susie!" I said. "I'm so glad you're here! I was afraid you might've gone back to your grave before we saw you again!"

"You aren't mad at us, are you?" asked Ollie. "I mean, 'cause we told you that your dad got married again?"

She shook her head. "I had a lot of thinkin' to do, after what y'all told me," she said. "But I reckon you was right, it *was* good news about my daddy gettin' away from Mr. Briggs. And he couldn't do nothin' to help Mama and me and Rebecca, so if he got married again, well, I hope he had a happy life."

"I didn't want you to be mad," said Ollie, "'cause you're our great-great…whatever…you're our auntie! Doesn't that rock?!"

Susie smiled. "I didn't *never* expect to hear nothin' like that! Just come as a surprise, is all. But a blessin' just the same…I got me a niece and a nephew."

"Yeah, look!" Ollie said. "We've got dimples, just like you!" He gave her a big grin and pointed to the dimples in his cheeks.

"Well, so you do," said Susie.

"So are you gonna go back to your grave?" he asked. "Is it like Granny said? Can you die satisfied now?"

She nodded. "No need for me to be here no more, but I had to say goodbye to y'all."

"But you could stay!" I said. "You could be my friend, and...and, like a sister! We could have lots of fun! Please?"

"And mine, too!" said Sofi. "I'd bring Coco for you to play with!"

"Yeah, you could stay here in my room!" said Ollie.

Susie looked around, then shook her head. "Y'all's makin' it hard for me, ya know? But I belong with my mama and baby sister."

"She's right, you know," said Sal. "She's gonna be twelve years old forever. The same reason Samuel couldn't stay with us."

I'd never thought anything would be as hard for me as when Samuel left, but I was wrong. I looked at Susie.

"Could you do one more thing for us?" I asked. "Remember how Sal wrote down your story of what it was like to be a slave? Well, I have to write a report, too, and I want to write about escaping on the underground railroad. So could you tell us what it was really like?"

"I want to hear it, too!" said Ollie.

"I reckon I could do that," she said.

"Hang on a sec," I said. I grabbed the quilt off of Ollie's bed and wrapped it around us, to keep warm.

Chapter 25
Susie's Harrowing Escape

Susie sat down in front of us. She closed her eyes and hugged her arms. Her face in the lamp light looked almost like she was in a trance.

"It was dark but there was some light from the moon. Mama come and wake me up, whisperin' to me to keep quiet. She tell me to put on my dress and apron and boots, and come with her down to the creek before the sun comes up. It was late summer, so the nights was gettin' longer.

"I followed Mama in the dark, down to the creek, listenin' to the crickets and locuses singin' in the night. I was afraid, 'cause I thought Mr. Chase's dogs might come after us.

"'Where we goin'?' I asked Mama, and she say she'll

tell me in a little bit, when it's safer. After about a mile, she turns to me and says we's runnin' away from Mr. Chase so's he can't sell me down south, like he selled my two brothers.

"I just followed my mama in the dark, stayin' close to the creek, hopin' she knew where we was goin'. I got tired of walkin' and started to whine a little, and Mama shushed me and said I gotta keep quiet. Somehow I kept goin' even though I just wanted to lay down and sleep.

"We walked on until the sun was startin' to come up, and I was glad I'd worn the boots instead of just goin' barefoot like usual. We looked around for a place we could sleep. We found a stand of pine trees, and Mama made a bed out of the needles on the ground. There was a deep place in the creek and we got some water to drink with the biscuits Mama brung. We couldn't make no fire 'cause the smoke would've give us away.

"I was hungry, but more'n that I was so tired I couldn't hardly keep my eyes open. But next thing I knows, Mama's shakin' me and whisperin' I gotta wake up, real quiet. She say we gotta go acrost the creek. She heared some dogs barkin' and she's afraid they's out lookin' for us.

"I was so scared I couldn't hardly move, but Mama say I can't cry, no matter what! So I got up and followed Mama into the creek. We walked a ways in the water till we got to a place where we could hide on the other side.

There was a big tree fell over with a lot of vines growin' around it, so we went and hid there. Mama didn't let me even say one word.

"Even though I was scared half to death, I was still so tired I just went to sleep. I guess if them dogs had found me, I would've just had to go back to Miz Chase. But they didn't find us. Mama told me when I woke up, she heared 'em barkin' and bayin' and she was almost scared to breathe, but they never picked up our scent, there acrost the creek.

"We stayed there by that dead tree the rest of the day. Mama give me an apple to eat when the sun gone down, and we got ready to walk again. We went on again all night, and I can't hardly remember much about it, just that it was dark, and I kept hearin' noises. I heared howlin' and thought the dogs was after us again, but Mama says it's just the coy-oats, and I wished I was back in the cabin with my sisters and not out there. But somehow we got through that night, too, and when the sun come up, we found another place to hide out for the day and sleep.

"That night we went back acrost the creek and headed up along a lot of trees. The moon was getting' fuller by then so we could see a bit. I was afraid of steppin' on a snake or somethin', but I never did."

"But how did you know where to go?" asked Ollie. "You didn't have a map or anything, did you?"

"I just followed Mama. She say she can tell where to go by lookin' at the stars. My daddy showed her this one star to look for, to tell which way's north. She say we just gotta go north."

"Sounds pretty scary!" said Ollie.

"So we walks again for another night, then Mama says we's close to the river. We went down by the water to wash off and rest a bit. I never seen a river this big before, and I hoped we didn't have to get in. We ate the last of our biscuits and apples, and found a place to hide for the day. I cried 'cause the food was all gone, but Mama told me to hush. I cried myself to sleep as the sun come up.

"Next thing I knows Mama's wakin' me up again. The sun was high in the sky, so I knows it wasn't time to start walkin' again. That's when I seen there was someone else with Mama. A white lady.

"Turns out, Mama was tired, too, but she went lookin' for somethin' for me to eat, 'cause she knowed I was so hungry. She seen flies buzzin' and found a patch of blackberries, and started pickin' 'em. Her hands was all bloody from the thorns and all, but she filled up her apron and was about to come back to our hidin' place, when this lady steps out from behind a tree and asks her what she's doin'."

"Oh, my gosh!" I exclaimed. I couldn't help it, I was so caught up in Susie's story.

"I seen this lady, and I start cryin' all over again, 'cause I was so scared she was gonna take us back to Mr. Chase. But she just says to Mama we should come with her to the barn, and stay there till the evenin' when her husband gets home, and they'll help get us to a safe place."

"YAYYYY!" I said, and we all clapped. Sal put his finger to his lips. Oops!

"So we go to the barn with the lady, Miz Hayes, her name was, and hid in a hoss stall, and she brung some food for us—milk and some more biscuits and even some butter! I couldn't hardly get enough! But Mama say we got to just stay hid 'til we knows what to do next.

"That evenin' Miz Hayes come out to the barn to bring some more food for us, and a blanket to wrap up in. We can't have no candles or fire in the barn, and it's mighty dark, but at least we has a roof over our heads. Miz Hayes told Mama we's in Kansas Territory now, but we still gotta be careful 'cause the Bushwhackers come sometimes to raid on the border. That's what they call them men what want to bring slavery to Kansas. The free-state fighters, they was called Jayhawkers.

"So we went up into the barn loft and hid out one more night, 'cause we didn't want no Bushwhackers findin' us, then the next day Mr. Hayes come out to the barn. He had a load of hay ready to take to town, and he helps me and Mama hide inside the hay. It was hot and dirty, and I couldn't hardly breathe, and I had to hold my nose to keep from sneezin.' Like to scare me to death, 'cause we couldn't even see where we's goin.'

"After a time we hear men talkin', and they say we's goin' acrost the river. I couldn't hardly keep from cryin' when we got on the water, but Mama held my hand and whispered to me. Then we got back on land and after while it got darker and quieter, so I knowed we was in a stable or somethin' like it. That's when Mr. Hayes told us it was safe to come out, and we dug our way outta that hay."

"Were you in Quindaro?" asked Ollie.

"Were you finally safe?" asked Sal.

"We was in a big, dark buildin' and that's where we seen Mr. Armstrong for the first time. He had a empty wagon with him and he and Mr. Hayes put the hay on that wagon, then me and Mama got back in the hay. Mr. Armstrong took us to the stable behind his house, and when it got dark, he come and took us in the house. And that's how we come to be with Mr. and Miz Armstrong."

Susie sighed and opened her eyes.

Chapter 26

One More Piece to the Puzzle

"You were finally safe!" I said.

Susie seemed to relax. "We was safe," she said. "Miz Armstrong was awful good to us. Lookin' back, seems like that shoulda been one of the best times of my life… and it was, 'cept for my daddy not bein' there. And Mama cryin' ever' night for weeks on account of leavin' my sisters and brother behind."

"I wish I could run away from *my* sister," said Ollie.

"Good idea," I said. "Why don't you?"

"Susie, that's one of the best stories I ever heard!" said Sal. "You were so brave!"

"But I feel so bad that you went through all that, and then died from the measles!" I said. "It just isn't fair!"

"Being a slave was the most unfair of all," said Sal.

He was right.

"Can't change things now," said Susie. "But the way I see it, y'all give *me* a gift. You give me the good news about my daddy, my old family, and then y'all say I got me a new family. So I come out of it all right."

"Are you really going back to your grave now?" I asked.

Susie nodded. "No need to wait for my daddy no more, now I knows he come and tried to find me."

"But I like hearing you sing!" said Sofi.

Susie smiled at Sofi. "Singin's always a joy for me, when I'm feelin' sad, or just thinkin' about the good times we used to have back when we was all together. Guess now I ought to sing 'cause *we's* all together…my new family I never knowed about."

It looked like Susie took a deep breath, but I'm not sure that's what she was doing, since ghosts probably don't breathe. Anyway, she looked up at the ceiling and started singing.

"Hey, that's a cool song!" said Ollie. And it was! Susie sang it again, this time clapping her hands and swaying from side to side. The words were so simple and the tune was so catchy, we all joined in, swaying and clapping. And watching ourselves in the mirror, seeing how weird and goofy we looked, we couldn't help but keep it up, getting louder and louder.

Suddenly I noticed Susie had stopped singing. She was just looking at us, and somehow I knew she was memorizing our faces. "Susie?" I said. "What is it?"

"It's time," she said. Everybody got quiet.

"Won't you miss us?" I asked.

"I surely will," said Susie. "I be sorry not to see y'all no more."

Then Sofi asked, "Will you ever come back?"

The way Susie looked right then made me get a lump in my throat. Honest, I think she wished she could stay with us.

"Y'all knows that's where I belong now, don't ya?" she said. "In my grave."

We all nodded. I was afraid to say anything, because I didn't want to cry, but all of a sudden, I remembered one of the questions I'd been wondering about.

"Susie…speaking of your grave…where is it? Do you know where you and your Mama and Rebecca were buried?" I asked.

"Out in the old Quindaro buryin' grounds," she said.

"Up on a hill, where you can see the river through the trees. A fittin' place, it was, 'cause acrost that river was freedom."

I had no idea where the Quindaro "burying grounds" were, but just knowing there was a real place made me feel a little better.

"Y'all take care of my things—my baby doll and my sewin' box," she said. "And don't forget to tell your granny 'thank you' for the news about my daddy…don't know how I can ever return the favor…promise me?"

"We will!" cried Ollie.

"And…most of all…keep me in your hearts."

"We promise!" we all said. Susie held up her hand and pushed her palm toward us, and we waved at the mirror. Even Butterscotch lifted her head off her paws and sniffed. She seemed to be looking up at something instead of in the mirror, but I was too sad at the thought of Susie leaving to wonder why. As we watched, Susie faded away.

Chapter 27

Susie's Sign

Over the weekend I knew I had to get to work on my report, but I didn't feel much like it, knowing Susie would never come back again. Saturday afternoon I sat on my bed staring at my notebook, but I couldn't write anything. I looked at the little humpback chest sitting by my desk and thought about Susie's doll. It was still in Ollie's room, where we'd left it last night. Suddenly I wanted to hold it.

I got to Ollie's door just as he was coming upstairs. We went in his room, where the doll was sitting on the floor in front of the mirror. As I leaned over to pick it up, I noticed a smudge on the mirror. I looked closer. It was definitely a handprint.

"Look," I said. "Did you put your dirty hand on the mirror?"

He came to look. "That's not mine," he said. "See, it's too big." He held his palm up near the mirror. "And anyway, I didn't touch it!"

"What about Sal or Sofi?" I asked.

"What?" he said. "It's way too big for Sofi, and Sal's hand's no bigger than mine! It was probably you! You touched it and you're trying to blame it on somebody else!"

By this time I was crouching down in front of the mirror, playing back the last scene with Susie in my head. The handprint was right where her hand was when she raised it to say goodbye to us.

"I think it's Susie's!" I cried. "Look—her hand was right here before she went away!" I held my palm up to the print. "And it's bigger than mine, too! You know what this means, don't you? Susie was really right here in the room with us!"

"Duh," said Ollie.

"No! I mean, not just in the mirror! She was *out here*—this is *real proof*!" I said.

"Oh, yeah," he said. "And hey, Butterscotch knew it! I remember now, she looked up, and not in the mirror, when Susie left—wow!"

"She was here with us and we didn't even know it!" I said.

I felt so much better after seeing Susie's handprint, I went back to my room and wrote a whole page of my report. I thought about all the things I'd learned about the underground railroad—from Wally and Betty, from Granny, and from Susie. I wrote about how dangerous and scary it would be to walk miles at night with no map and listening for dogs barking and noises in the night. I put in some lines about the station at Quindaro, right across the river from where I live. In my mind I replayed the look on Susie's face as she told us about the journey to Kansas. My report was going to be great!

We told Sal and Sofi about the handprint later that afternoon.

"I wonder what was different last night," said Sal. "How she could be out in the room with us?"

We took them to Ollie's room to see the handprint.

"I think Susie wanted to give us something," I said. "Something we can see, even if she went back to her grave, like Samuel's woodcarvings."

"It's because she knows we love her," said Sofi.

"Don't wipe it off!" Ollie said. "I want to leave it there forever."

I finished my report about the underground railroad, and felt really good about it. Sal thought Mr. Franklin would really like his report about the work that slave kids had to do. We left the doll sitting on the floor of Ollie's room, but Susie never came back. I hoped we would hear her singing some time, just to know she was somehow still nearby, but we never did. The doll finally got covered up by a dirty T-shirt and some toys.

I pinned Susie's sampler to my bulletin board. Mom asked me where I got it, and who Birdie and Ezekiel were. I told her about the humpback chest and the diary in Granny's locker and the story of Granny's great-grandpa. But I didn't give away Susie's—or Granny's—secret.

Chapter 28

A Last Visit with Granny

One warm spring afternoon when we came into the kitchen after school, Mom was waiting to meet us. She looked sad. "Granny had a stroke," she said.

"What's a stroke?" asked Ollie. "Is it real bad?"

"It is," said Mom. "She's paralyzed. That means she can't move or talk, and we don't know if she can hear us or understand us."

"Is she gonna die?" I asked. We'd been so busy, we hadn't visited Granny again after we told Susie about her dad coming to Kansas. I'd promised Susie I would thank Granny for the news.

"We don't know," said Mom, "but it's possible. She's 94, after all."

"Are we ever gonna see her again?" asked Ollie.

"We can go see her," she said, "but just for a few minutes."

A couple of days later, Mom took us to visit Granny. After her stroke, she had to go to a place where they could feed her and give her baths and everything. Before we got there, Mom warned us that Granny would be hooked up to some machines that might look scary, and she might not even open her eyes or know we were there.

The sign in front of the building said "nursing and rehabilitation." There were long hallways with lots of rooms and it smelled pretty awful. The room Granny was in was gray and gloomy, with no pictures on the wall or anything. Like Mom said, Granny had tubes coming out of her nose and another tube stuck into her arm. She looked like she was asleep. I wished we hadn't come.

Mom went right up to Granny's bed. "Hi, Granny," she said. "I have a surprise! Orion and Ollie are here to see you!" Granny didn't open her eyes or move or any-thing. It was weird, hearing Mom talk to her and she didn't even answer. I wanted to leave, and I could tell Ollie felt the same way, but Mom pulled us both up close to the bed. She kept talking, telling Granny about how the house was ready to sell, and how it looked so nice and clean, with the flowers blooming. Then she said, "I'll bet Granny would like to hear your voices."

Ollie and I looked at each other. What were we sup-posed to say? I'd never seen anyone who'd had a stroke before. Just a few days ago she'd been sitting in her chair and talking to us, and now I couldn't even tell if she was alive. "Uh, hi, Granny," I mumbled.

It's hard to believe, but sometimes my brother knows exactly what to do. He leaned over close to Granny and said, "Granny, I sure liked seeing the medals my great-grandpa got in the war. Could I see them again? Maybe Grandpa will show them to me."

He was right. *Just talk to Granny like we always did.* I leaned closer to her ear.

"I loved hearing you tell about your grandma's diary!" I said. "And I hope we can see it again, too…and the har-monica…I want to learn all about our family history!"

"I'll bet Grandpa can tell you a lot," said Mom.

"You know, Granny," I said, "everything you told us was so amazing! I wrote my report for school about the underground railroad, and my teacher loved it!"

"And I love the mirror from the attic!" said Ollie. "It's about the awesomest thing I've ever had!"

Mom picked up Granny's hand, the one that didn't have the tube sticking into it, and said, "I'll bet she'd like to hold your hands."

I wasn't sure about that, but again, Ollie stepped up. He put his hand over Mom's, and she slipped her hand away so that he was gripping Granny's fingers. Well, if my little brother could do this, so could I! I took hold of Granny's hand. I thought about all the things she'd told us, about Ezekiel and her house and the secrets she'd kept, and how she'd never gotten to see or talk to Susie. I don't know what made me do it, but I started singing.

Rock-a my soul in the bosom of Abraham, rock-a my soul in the bosom of Abraham…

Ollie picked up the song with me.

Rock-a my soul in the bosom of Abraham, oh, rock-a my soul!

It sounds weird, but singing the song, I could almost feel Susie in the room with us. I hoped that somehow Granny could feel it, too, even though she was stuck in that awful place and couldn't even open her eyes.

Right then a nurse came to the door and told Mom it was time to check Granny's vital signs. Mom went to talk to the nurse for a minute, so I leaned in close to Granny and whispered in her ear, "We told Susie about Ezekiel. She says 'thank you.'"

Ollie leaned in beside me and whispered, "If you hadn't told us your secret, she never would've known… and now she's part of our family, and we gave her your love. She—" His head jerked up before he could say any more. I knew from the look on his face that he felt what I had just felt! Granny had squeezed my fingers! Right then I knew she could hear us and she understood that Susie had died satisfied and gone back to her grave. We both squeezed her fingers tighter and sang through the song once more.

"We need to go now," said Mom as the nurse came over to Granny's bed. Ollie and I let go of her hand. "Bye, Granny," we said, and followed Mom out of the room.

MOM SEEMED SAD ON THE WAY HOME. She didn't say much, but she did ask us where we learned that song.

"Uh, I don't know," I said. "Just picked it up somewhere."

After dinner that night, Grandpa Louie called and talked to Mom. She came upstairs and called me over to Ollie's room. Her eyes looked red and I had a bad feeling about what she was going to say.

"Grandpa just called to tell us that Granny died this afternoon," she said. "I told him about our visit and how you were so sweet to her. I was so proud of both of you!" Mom gave us each a hug.

"Is Grandpa feeling sad?" asked Ollie.

"He is," said Mom, "but Granny had a good, long life. Grandpa said she died peacefully, and she seemed to have a little smile on her face. I'm sure she was glad you came to see her."

"I'm glad, too," said Ollie.

Mom hugged us again and I went back to my room. Funny, I was thinking how Ollie had helped me get through the visit to Granny. I never thought I'd have to admit he's better at something than I am, but he is. He's the reason we had that special moment with Granny.

Maybe someday I'll tell him.

Granny was going to be cremated. Mom said that's when they burn your body in a real hot furnace and all that's left is some ashes, like in the fireplace after the wood burns down. They give the ashes to the dead person's family.

"Why would anybody want to keep the ashes?" asked Ollie. "That's creepy!"

"Yeah," I said. "I mean, Granny's gone, so what good are some ashes?"

"Well, sometimes people scatter the ashes somewhere that the dead person loved," said Mom. "That way, the person becomes a part of that place."

"That's better than keeping them!" said Ollie. "Is Grandpa going to scatter Granny's ashes somewhere?"

"I think so," said Mom. "He and his sisters are thinking of where the best place would be."

Chapter 29

Ollie's Accident

The Friday before Ollie's birthday, a couple weeks before school was out, we were in the back yard with Sal and Sofi. Coco, who had grown a lot since Sofi brought her home, was nosing around in the grass. She probably smelled a rabbit or something. I was working with Butterscotch to get her to run the sticks on command.

Ollie and Sal were on the treehouse platform, getting ready to swing to the trapeze bar. Sal went first, grabbing the bar as he let go of the rope. He swung back and forth on the bar a few times, then dropped to the ground.

Ollie went next. "Geronimo!" he yelled as he sailed over our heads. I wasn't really watching, since I'd seen him try it a bazillion times, but out of the corner of my eye I suddenly realized Ollie was on the ground and not moving. I looked over, frozen in my tracks. Sal and Sofi stood stock-still, looking shocked. *Oh, no*, I thought, *is he dead*?

All at once, Ollie screamed, "OOWWWW!"

I came to my senses and ran to the house, yelling, "MOM!!"

MOM AND DAD BROUGHT OLLIE HOME from the emergency room with a splint on his arm. It wasn't a real bad break, they said, but he'd have to wear the splint for a few weeks until his arm healed. He was whimpering about the pain and whining about not getting to practice his Ninja Warrior moves.

With all the excitement, it was pretty late by the time we got ready for bed. Dad helped Ollie get a shirt on to sleep in. The doctor gave him some medicine to help with the pain so he could sleep.

The next day was Saturday, so Dad was home, and he and Mom spent every minute fussing over Ollie. Sal and Sofi brought him some of their mom's biscotti. Grandma and Grandpa came and brought him a new book. They always give us books for our birthdays and Christmas.

Ollie slept a lot that day, so it was actually pretty peaceful for me, but I *did* feel sorry for him. That night, after I got my pajamas on, I went to his room, and he asked if I'd read to him from his new book. I used to read to him a lot when he was little, and I hadn't done it for a while, so I settled in on the foot of his bed, leaning on a pillow.

"Orion?" he said. "I had a dream about Susie last night."

"You did?" I asked. "What happened?"

"Well, she was singing that 'Rock-a my soul' song. I listened for a while, then went back to sleep. But it had to be a dream, didn't it?" he asked.

"Yeah, I'm pretty sure," I said. "I don't think she'll ever come back again." To be honest, I'd be really mad if she came back to see Ollie but not me. "Did she say anything to you?"

"No, I don't think so…I don't remember," he said.

I opened the book and started to read. It was about a boy who broke his leg and had to go to the hospital. Ollie had taken more medicine and by the end of the first chapter, he was out like a light. I sat for a minute thinking about what he'd said about his dream. I didn't realize I'd fallen asleep until I woke up in the dark. Somebody had put a blanket over me and turned out the light. Ollie was whispering to me.

"Orion? Listen!"

"What? What's wrong?" I asked.

"Don't you hear that?" he said. "Somebody's singing!"

"I don't hear any—" I started, then I stopped.

Rock-a my soul in the bosom of Abraham, rock-a my soul in the bosom of Abraham…

"Oh, my God!" I cried. "Is it Susie?" I jumped up and turned on Ollie's lamp, then scrambled over to the mirror in the corner of his room.

"Susie? Are you there?" I asked. I waited, hardly daring to breathe. In a moment, I saw Susie's shining eyes and dimpled cheeks. I looked over at Ollie. "She's here!" I whispered.

"My arm hurts!" said Ollie. "I don't know if I can get out of bed!"

I had an idea. As quietly as I could, I scooted the mirror closer to Ollie's bed, so it faced him. "Can you see her?" I asked. I came around and sat on the edge of the bed.

"Hi, Susie," said Ollie. "I broke my arm!" He held his splint up for her to see.

"Now why'd y'all go and do that?" she asked. "I was almost all settled back in my grave, when I got this feelin' y'all needed me…I didn't know what for."

"You came back, just to see me?" said Ollie. I'd never seen him look that happy!

"Thought I better look in on ya, make sure y'all's all right," she said.

Ollie was sitting up now. He was so psyched, I think he forgot how much his arm was hurting. He told Susie all about how he broke it.

"Just like my brothers!" said Susie. "Them little boys is such rascals!"

We all laughed.

"Susie, does this mean you're not gonna stay in your grave?" asked Ollie. "Will you come back to be with us now?"

Susie shook her head. "Now y'all knows I cain't do that, don't ya?"

"Yeah, I guess so," he said, looking disappointed. "Did you know our granny died? Ms. Bets?" he asked. "So now we're the only ones who know the secret of the house in Quindaro."

"And Sal and Sofi," I added.

"I'm right sorry to hear she died," said Susie. "But my secret's done now. Don't nobody have to pass it on no more."

"You mean this is the last time we'll see you?" I asked.

Susie nodded. "Y'all don't know how hard it is...not just the comin' back, but the leavin', too."

"Can you stay just a little while longer?" Ollie asked. "Could you sing more songs to me?"

She smiled. "I reckon I could do that," she said.

So, Susie sang the songs she'd learned from her family, and Ollie nestled into his pillow and closed his eyes. The last song she sang was the old lullaby.

Hush-a-bye, don't you cry, go to sleepy, little baby...

Ollie's not a baby, but right then, it was just the right thing. I looked at him in the lamp light, and I could tell he'd fallen asleep. Susie knew it, too.

"My time here's over," she said. "Gotta go back to be with my own baby sister. But I'm countin' on y'all to take good care of this young'un. Try showin' a little patience. What if y'all was never gonna see him again, ever? Like my brothers."

"Excuse me? You don't know what a pain in the butt—" I started, but then I stopped. I suddenly saw, through Susie's eyes, a bossy girl who's always trash-talking her younger brother. I felt embarrassed, and a little ashamed.

"I'm sorry, Susie," I said. "You're right. And I really feel bad for Ollie 'cause he broke his arm…."

"It ain't easy, bein' the oldest," she said. "I oughta know. But ya gotta be the best sister you can. Promise?"

"I promise," I said.

Ollie slept on, looking so peaceful I got a lump in my throat. I hadn't realized how worried I'd been about him since the accident.

"I know I boss Ollie around a lot. I'll really try to do better!" I said.

"I knows ya will," said Susie. "Now I hates goodbyes, so I'll just say, 'til we meet again.'"

"I'll never, ever, forget you!" I said, but she was gone before I even finished.

Chapter 30
Susie's Final Resting Place

 I woke up the next morning to my dad's voice calling, "Orion! Ollie! Pancakes for breakfast! Time to wake up!"

I turned over and pulled my blanket over my head. I just wanted to go back to sleep. Then I opened my eyes. I was in my own bed. *Wait, wasn't I in Ollie's room last night? And didn't Susie come and see us?* I jumped out of bed and went straight to Ollie's room. He blinked a few times when I sat on his bed. He started to sit up, forgetting about the splint, but then fell back to his pillow.

"You won't believe what I dreamed!" he said. "Susie was here, and she sang to me, and…"

"SHHH!" I said. "Are you sure it was a dream? Didn't I come in and read to you last night?"

"Uh, yeah," he said. "There's my new book that

Grandpa and Grandma gave me. I guess I fell asleep while you were reading."

"That's what I thought! And then I fell asleep, and I remember you woke me up, and we heard Susie singing, and she came to talk to us. But this morning I woke up in my own bed!"

I looked around Ollie's room, and saw the mirror in the corner, where it had always been. Hadn't I moved it closer to his bed?

"What else did Susie say?" I asked. "In your dream?"

"Um, she felt bad that I broke my arm…and we told her Granny died…that's really all I remember."

"That's what I remember too," I said, "but then you went to sleep, and she told me some more stuff."

"What?" he asked.

"Oh, just…that she hates to say goodbye," I said. Now I was wondering if it *was* all a dream. But Susie's words were so clear to me…

"I feel a lot better now!" Ollie said suddenly.

We heard Dad coming up the stairs. He came in with a tray and set it on Ollie's desk. He helped Ollie sit up and sat beside him, holding the tray while Ollie ate his pancakes.

"I want some!" I whooped, and ran down to the kitchen to get some before they were all gone.

Later that afternoon Ollie was out of bed and running around the house. I guess his arm didn't hurt much, because he was acting as dumb as ever. We went out to the back yard to watch Butterscotch run her obstacle course.

"I'm gonna tell Sal about my dream!" he said. "About how Susie sang songs to me!"

"Really?" I said. "I was thinking maybe it should be our secret—just you and me, you know?"

"But he always told us about his dreams of Samuel," he said.

"You can tell him if you want," I said. "About *your* dream. But I'm keeping mine...if it was a dream...for myself."

The next week, on Ollie's ninth birthday, Grandma and Grandpa came over for dinner. We took them to the back yard to show them Butterscotch's obstacle course. I let Ollie take her through the sticks and jump over the hurdle.

They gave Ollie a robot-building kit, and Mom and Dad got him a new Lego kit. Dad also told him his brother, our Uncle Jeff, was going to help build a salmon ladder. He said it'd probably be finished by the time Ollie's splint comes off. The best thing, though, was that Grandpa brought the medals. He let Ollie take them out of the box and helped him pin them on his shirt. Mom snapped pictures of him on her phone.

"Grandpa," asked Ollie, "where are you going to scatter Granny's ashes?"

"Good question," said Grandpa. "I've been talking about it with my sisters, and we want to do it somewhere that would mean a lot to Granny."

"Well, I have an idea," I said. "What about the old Quindaro burying ground?"

"How do you know about that?" asked Grandma.

"From Granny," I said.

"Do you know where it is?" asked Ollie.

"The Old Quindaro Cemetery's not far from Granny's house," said Grandma, "but it's hardly used any more. It's hidden away in the trees and hard to find."

"Can you see the river from on top of a hill?" asked Ollie.

"I haven't been there in years," said Grandpa. "You could probably see the river when the trees have lost their leaves. It's kind of spooky. I went there on Halloween a couple of times when I was a kid. I don't remember ever hearing Granny talk about it. Why do you think she would want her ashes to be there?"

I had to think fast. "Well, you know that diary that was in the footlocker?" I said. "Granny told us about what her grandma wrote in it, and it made me think of slaves who ran away and came here back then. And then

I heard that some of them might have been buried in the Quindaro graveyard."

"As I remember it," said Grandpa, "it's mostly just a big empty space hidden back in the trees. There's hardly even any gravestones."

"But that doesn't matter, does it?" I asked. "Granny told us her great-grandpa was a slave, and if there are slaves buried there, wouldn't it be a good place for her ashes?"

Grandpa looked thoughtful. "Hmmm," he said, "I'll talk to my sisters about it. Memorial Day's coming up, and that's when I was thinking about scattering the ashes."

"Can we go?" asked Ollie.

"We should all go," said Mom.

THE NEXT WEEKEND, Grandpa called and told Mom he and his sisters had decided to scatter Granny's ashes at the Old Quindaro cemetery. They liked my idea about connecting her with the old slave burial grounds.

"He told me they talked about the diary that was in Granny's footlocker," said Mom. "He'd never really looked at it before, but after you kids talked to Granny about it, he asked her to tell him what she knew about the family history. He thinks we really might have ancestors buried at Old Quindaro."

"I knew it!" cried Ollie.

"Really?" said Mom. "Anyway, we'll go out there on Memorial Day. I know you said Sal and Sofi want to go, because they knew about the diary, too."

"And they visited Granny too," I said. "This way we can all say goodbye to her together."

Chapter 31
Memories of Susie

Isn't it funny how all year you can't wait for school to be out, but when it finally is, you think of all the things you're going to miss? Fifth grade had been an amazing year, but the last day finally came. Mom helped me color my hair purple—*all* my hair, not just streaks—and it looked awesome! She says I'll have to wash it out before we go to the pool for the first time, though. Mady and Taylor both dyed their hair with Jell-O. Mady's blonde, and she used lime, and it turned out perfect, but Taylor's got black hair, so the red Jell-O didn't show up much.

I'd had a good year with Ms. Patel. She talked to us about all the different things we'd learned, then we divided into teams and had a contest to see who could remember the most. My team lost, but Ms. Patel gave everybody candy at the end. She also had us all share something important that we'd always remember from fifth grade. That was a hard one for me. I had a lot to choose from. I ended up saying that I'd learned my great-great-great-great grandfather was a slave.

I'd also learned a lot from Mr. Franklin in the accelerated math class. He added up the scores of all our quizzes and practices for everyone in the class, and I came in 7th highest out of the twelve kids. Sal had the best score (no surprise), but the second-high score was a girl. Mady came in 4th and Taylor was 8th, which proved to me that girls are just as good at math as boys. I'm looking forward to doing the class again in sixth grade.

For our last gym class, Miss Henderson staged a mini-track meet. I could tell my training had paid off. I won the 100-meter race for our grade and came in second in the 50-meter. Miss Henderson said it's because I'm conditioned to keep up my speed for the longer runs. I'm going to get even better by next year!

Mom picked us up from school the last day because we all had so much to bring home. She picked up Sal and Sofi, too, because their mom was working that day. Before we left, she snapped pictures of me, Mady and Taylor with our colored hair.

On the way home, Ollie said, "I heard Micah Fitzwater tell you he liked your hair! I bet he wants to go out with you!" He laughed and made a smoochie face at me, which Mom couldn't see.

He was in the back seat with Sal, where I couldn't pound him, so I just mouthed, "Shut up!" The truth is, Micah's kind of cute.

"Orion's not going out with anybody," said Mom.

"He's the shortstop on my baseball team," said Sal.

Really? Maybe I ought to go with Sofi to some of those baseball games this summer...

THAT FIRST NIGHT AFTER SCHOOL WAS OUT, Mom said we could stay up late. I watched TV for a while, then went up to my room and thought about what a strange year it had been. This time last year I didn't believe in ghosts. I believed Mom when she said there's a reasonable explanation for everything. And now I've met two ghosts in person!

I thought about Susie and all I learned from her. She never went to school, or even learned to read, but she could do so many things! She was only a year older than me, but she could make clothes, weave cloth, grow food, and take care of little kids. She and Samuel were sort of alike in that way. He only went to school for two years, but he learned how to build houses and make furniture, and he could hunt and fish for food. If I was stuck on an island with just two other people, who would I want them to be? Not Mady and Taylor—I love them both, but they wouldn't know how to keep us alive. I'll take Samuel and Susie any day!

I thought about the way Susie looked at the world, and how strong she was. She lived a horrible, hard life. I wondered if I could be as brave and responsible as she was. What would it be like to be afraid you might be sold away from your parents? What if you had someone telling you what to do, all day, every day? But even worse, what if you knew you'd be a slave your whole life? You couldn't dream of what you'd be when you grew up. You didn't have any choices about your own life! Susie never got to choose what she wanted to be, but instead of hating her owners (like I would have), she focused on the love of her family.

And don't tell Ollie, but I thought about what she said to me about being a good sister. And it reminded me of something Samuel Grayhawk had told us: he said it was a sister's job to help their brothers grow up to be good men. Samuel loved his sister so much—I don't think Ollie feels that way about me! But what if I never saw my little brother again? Maybe Sal was right, I should start cutting him some slack. After all, I'm in sixth grade now, way more grown-up than he is.

I thought about Granny, and was a little sad that we only started to really get to know her. But it was so cool that we did! What if we hadn't gone to help clean her house? What if we'd never looked in the mirror? What if

Granny had never told us about the diary and the secret in the attic? Susie might still be waiting for her dad to come, and never be able to die satisfied. I think Granny died satisfied, too, knowing how she'd helped Susie.

Maybe Mom's right—there's a reason it rained over spring break. Everything that happened led us to helping Susie die satisfied and go to her grave. I can't explain it, but I believe it.

Chapter 32

Memorial Day

I was hoping Memorial Day would be sunny and warm for our trip to the Old Quindaro cemetery, but it was cloudy with a chilly wind. Mom said we had to get going early to scatter Granny's ashes, because it might rain later. Grandpa and Grandma came over to pick us all up—Mom, me, Ollie, Sal and Sofi.

When we got to the entrance of the cemetery, I thought we were out in a forest or something. There wasn't even a real road, just a dirt trail with trees all around. The stormy weather made it seem kind of creepy, and Sofi looked a little scared. It seemed like we drove through the trees for miles, but finally we came to a clearing at the side of a hill and Grandpa parked beside some concrete steps. We piled out of the van and ran up the grassy hill.

Grandpa was right. It didn't even look like a cemetery, just a big open space on a couple of hilltops. An old tree stood at the top of one of the hills. It had branches sticking out at weird angles and vines growing all over it.

"They say that's the Signal Tree," said Grandpa. "It's supposed to be a marker the slaves could see and know they made it to freedom."

"Wow, it must be really old!" said Sal. We ran to the tree and looked all around while Mom, Grandpa and Grandma walked over to the next hill.

"Can you see the river?" asked Ollie. We all looked toward the line of trees down a slope from the hilltop, but I didn't see any water.

Suddenly Sofi cried, "There it is!" We all crouched down to her level and looked where she was pointing. A bit of gray water showed through a break in the trees.

"I see it!" I said. "I bet Susie was buried right around here!"

Sal looked around. "Maybe. Let's look from up there." We raced up the next hill where we found a few gravestones, but we couldn't see the river from there. "It's gotta be by the tree," he said.

Right then Mom called to us and said they were ready to scatter Granny's ashes. Grandpa was holding the little box the ashes were in. It was so weird that all that was left of Granny could fit in the box. All of us, even Sal and Sofi, took some of the ashes.

"Throw them in this direction," said Grandpa, "so the wind will carry them over the grounds."

We all threw our ashes and watched the wind carry them away.

"Rest in peace in this beautiful place, Mama," said Grandpa.

Everybody was quiet for a minute, then I asked, "Grandpa, what's the river you can see from the hill by the tree?"

"That's the Missouri," he said. "It comes all the way from up in Montana."

"Why would slaves say the river meant freedom?" asked Ollie.

"Because it led to the north," said Grandpa. "Nebraska, the Dakotas, and on up to Canada, that was free territory. The river was probably a powerful symbol for the slaves."

I understood why Susie would think this was a good place to be buried.

The wind got stronger and dark clouds rolled across the sky. Grandma said it was time to go.

"Can we just go back to the tree for a minute?" asked Ollie.

"Make it quick, and meet us at the car," said Mom.

We ran back to the Signal Tree. The wind whipped at

our jackets, and was so loud we could hardly hear each other, so we knelt on the ground.

"I think Susie's here," said Sofi.

"I wish we had something special to do for her, like how Samuel buried the marbles for his sister," said Sal.

"I know," I said. "But what?"

"Let's sing her a song," said Sofi. She looked at Ollie and they started in on a verse of "Rock-a My Soul."

Sal and I joined in, then I looked up at the tree and yelled, "Bye, Susie!" The others yelled goodbye to her, too. I took one last look at the river through the treetops. Just as I turned to head for the car, the wind died for a minute and I felt sunshine on my head. We all stopped and looked up as the sun broke through the clouds.

Ollie pumped his fist in the air. "Susie heard us!" he yelled. His face was shining, and I suddenly realized what Susie had meant to him. Then the sun went behind the clouds and the rain started as we ran to the car.

On the way home, Grandpa drove to the place where the town of Quindaro used to be. We looked through the rain down a long, steep grassy hill that led to the river, with lots of trees all around. You couldn't tell there was ever a town there. Like Susie, I thought, it's just a memory.

Epilogue

When we got home, Grandma and Grandpa stayed for a while, and Sal and Sofi went home. I started to go to my room, when Mom said, "Grandpa's got something to give you."

"I hope it's Granny's medals!" said Ollie.

"No, he's keeping those, but don't worry, they're staying in the family," said Mom. "Come to the family room and see."

Grandma and Grandpa were waiting for us in the family room. Grandpa was holding the diary from Granny's footlocker.

"Orion, Ollie, I want to thank you for bringing this diary to Granny's attention," he said. "Oh, she knew about it already, but she hadn't really thought about it in years. And to be honest, I'd never read it.

"But after Granny moved in with us, and you kids found the diary in the footlocker, she got me to read it to her. I learned things about the family I'd never known before, and I got to talk to my mom about them before she died. So I want you to know how much I appreciate it."

Oh, no! I thought. *I hope Granny didn't tell Grandpa we saw Susie's spirit!*

"What did she tell you about the family?" asked Ollie.

"Oh, we mostly talked about what was in the diary," said Grandpa. "She talked about her great-grandpa and how he escaped from slavery, and came to Kansas looking for his wife and daughter. Unfortunately, they died before he got here. But that's a fascinating piece of history to keep in the family."

Whew! It sounded like she didn't tell him about the secret of the attic room, or the rumors of the girl singing.

"Anyway," Grandpa went on, "Granny wanted you to have something to remind you of our family's history." He held out a harmonica—not the rusty, grimy one I remembered from the footlocker, but one that was shiny and silver and sparkled in the light.

"Wow!" said Ollie as he took the harmonica from Grandpa. He blew into it and it made a carnival-like sound, and I tried it, too.

"It was Granny's idea," he said. "It was handed down

from her great-grandpa, but nobody knew how to play it, so it just got packed away in the locker," said Grandpa.

"You mean this is the one from the locker?" I said. "The old rusty one?" With everything else going on, I'd forgotten all about it!

"I had to polish it up a bit," he said, "but it looks as good as new, don't you think?"

"Thanks, Grandpa!" I said. "This is so cool!"

He gave us each a hug. "It made her so happy to have you and your friends visit her. Just remember how old it is, and take good care of it."

"We will!" I promised. We ran upstairs to look on YouTube for how to play a harmonica. It's a lot harder than it looks, we found out.

WE SETTLED INTO SUMMER, with the pool, and friends, and taking it easy. Ollie got his splint off and started practicing on the new salmon ladder. I kept running at the playground, and after Dad timed me with a stopwatch, he took me to buy real running shoes. Sal hung out more with his buds on the baseball team and I spent my time with Mady and Taylor (and Sofi, of course, whenever she wanted). I didn't mind. Fifth grade was a special year, but it's time to move on.

The afternoon of Sal's eleventh birthday, Ollie and I went over to take him our gift. He was still a die-hard Mets fan (even though he'd lived in Kansas almost a year), so I'd made a poster-size drawing of the Mets logo, and Ollie had helped me color it in. We were pretty proud of it, and Sal really liked it. We went up to his room so he could decide where to put it, and that's when I unrolled another drawing I wanted him to see.

"It's Susie!" cried Sofi, and Sal looked at me in surprise.

"I knew you were good at drawing, but this is really great!" he said. "It looks exactly like her!"

"I made this one from memory, with her smiling and showing her dimples," I said. "I wanted something to remember her by."

"You have her doll and her sewing chest," said Sal. "And the harmonica."

"And the mirror!" said Ollie.

"And her songs!" said Sofi.

"That's right," I said, and I realized Susie's voice, and her songs, are just as real for us as something you can touch and hold. I know none of us will ever forget them.

"So," said Sal, "do you think we'll ever see another ghost?"

I thought for a minute and then said, "I don't know...and as much as I loved Samuel and Susie, it was so hard when they went away...I'm not sure I could stand that again."

"Yeah, I know what you mean," said Sal. "And what are the odds? I mean, even once was incredible. That's why I didn't believe in Susie at first."

"Well, Samuel and Susie were the coolest things that ever happened to me," piped up Ollie, "and I wish we'd see just *one* more!"

"Huh," said Sal, "my dad says you better be careful what you wish for."

Guess what? I didn't know it then, but Sal's dad was *so* right!

Afterword

Places and Terms

Quindaro was chartered as a city in 1857 by settlers who wanted a free-state port of entry into Kansas Territory. Located on the south bank of the Missouri River, it was named for Nancy Quindaro Brown, a Wyandot woman who came with her people from Ohio. The population of Quindaro included Native Americans and abolitionists from the east. There are many legends of runaway slaves arriving there by way of the Underground Railroad.

The Fugitive Slave Act of 1850 was a law passed by Congress that allowed slave owners (or their agents) to travel into other states or territories in pursuit of runaway slaves. It also provided for punishment for anyone helping slaves escape or hindering the owners' efforts to recover them.

The Wyandott House was a hotel opened in Quindaro by Ebenezer O. Zane. Mr. Zane was arrested in 1861 or 1862, accused of aiding runaway slaves. He was imprisoned until a bond of $1000 was paid. Mr. Zane's descendants still live in the area and have contributed vital information for the Orion O'Brien stories.

Another business rumored to be associated with

the Underground Railroad was the Zehntner-Steiner Brewery. Legends say there was a shaft inside the brewery through which ice could be brought up from the river. The shaft, approximately 20 inches square, was also used as a secret entry for runaway slaves arriving by boat. The brewery's ruins are the only structure surviving from the original town.

The 761st Tank Battalion, also known as the Black Panthers, was a unit of the U.S. Army deployed in Europe in 1944-45 near the end of World War II. The 761st assisted in breaking through the Siegfried Line into Germany and saw action at the Battle of the Bulge. Members of the battalion were almost all Black enlisted men, though their officers were all white. More than 300 citations were awarded to members of the 761st.

The Purple Heart and Bronze Star are medals awarded to members of the United States military services. The Purple Heart is awarded to those wounded or killed; the Bronze Star is awarded for heroic or meritorious achievement or service in a military conflict.

Kansas entered the Union as a free state in 1861 after several years of bloodshed along the border with Missouri. The Kansas-Nebraska Act of 1854 called for residents to decide whether Kansas would become a slave state or a free state. Skirmishes and battles resulted in deaths on both sides, earning the territory the name 'Bleeding Kansas.'

'Haint' is a word reputed to have originated with the Gullah, descendants of African slaves living on the Atlantic Coast of the United States. It often refers to evil spirits.

Calico cats are *almost* always female. There have been a few reported instances of male calico cats.

"Hush-a-bye," "Wade in the Water," and "Rock-a-my Soul" are all folk songs attributed to slaves in the American South. Though all have been arranged and performed by modern artists, they were passed down through generations of African American singers.

Samplers were made by stitching letters and pictures on fabric with needle and thread. The alphabet, numerals, and Bible verses were common subjects of samplers, as were flowers and animals. Different types of stitches were worked into the pictures, and they may have even been used to teach children to read. Young girls copied the stitches from their mothers' or other elder women's work, then practiced on their own samplers.

References and Sources

Information on the underground railroad
was obtained from Warren, Kim. "Seeking the
Promised Land: African American Migrations
to Kansas" *Civil War on the Western Border: The
Missouri-Kansas Conflict, 1854-1865.* https://
civilwaronthewesternborder.org/essay/seeking-
promised-land-africa... and from O'Bryan, Tony.
"Quindaro, Kansas" *Civil War on the Western Border:
The Missouri-Kansas Conflict, 1854-1865.* https://
civilwaronthewesternborder.org/encyclopedia/
quindaro-kansas

Information on the lives of slaves was obtained
from *Born in Slavery: Slave Narratives from the Federal
Writers' Project, 1936 to 1938*, available from the
Library of Congress at https://www.loc.gov/collections/
slave-narratives-from-the-federal-writers-project-
1936-to-1938. This is also the source of the slave saying,
"if you don't die satisfied, you have to come back."

Information on the ferries running in Wyandotte
County was obtained from The Kansas Historical
Quarterly, vol. 2, no. 3, August 1933, Ferries in Kansas,
Part II, Kansas River by George A. Root, pp. 251-293.
Kansas Historical Society website at https://www.kshs.
org/p/kansas-historical-quarterly-ferries-in-kansas-
part-ii-kansas-river/17493

Detailed information about Quindaro, including the businesses and families that formed the town, was obtained at https://www.kshs.org/kansapedia/quindaro/15163 (The Kansas Historical Society) and at https://legendsofkansas.com/quindaro-kansas/

About the Author

As a child growing up in eastern Kansas, Fran Borin eagerly soaked up stories from grandparents and family elders about the turbulent, sometimes violent history of the area. Bleeding Kansas and the Border War were well-known items of the local culture. While researching her first book, *Orion O'Brien and the Ghost of Samuel Grayhawk*, she was struck by the integral connection of Native Americans with the Underground Railroad. The historic site of Quindaro, just minutes from her home, provided the perfect setting for *Orion O'Brien and the Spirit of Quindaro*.

Fran lives with her husband within walking distance of the Shawnee Indian Mission. She has three grown children.